ORANGE

An Anthology Of Short Works By
Authors From Inspirations Writers'
Group, Thanet.

Published by Wayside Publications
Manston, Kent CT12 5AW
Paperback ISBN: 978-0-9933174-5-3

CONTENTS

FOREWORD

Welcome to the 'Orange Anthology', the second publication from the Inspirations Writers Group.

2017 has held many firsts for this hard-working group of writers. In January, we produced and launched our very first publication, the 'Red Anthology'. This publication received excellent feedback and acclaim, and at one-point demand outstripped supply. This successful book is still available as an e-book on all popular platforms, and as a paperback on Amazon and via our website; inspirationswritersgroup.weebly.com

Following on from this positive launch, the group formalised its structure, which included membership of the 'National Association of Writers' Groups'.

In May, we were nominated by a panel of judges as finalists for 'Community Organisation of the Year' in this year's Kent Creative Awards and achieved Runner-up status.

'Inspirations' is a group of people who write because it is part of their psyche, it is *who they are.* I am proud to know them and be part of this experience. At meetings, through their work, each member shares a part of themselves. They are prepared to accept comments and feedback on their writing in the knowledge that it will improve their writing ability. As a result, their work brings readers moments of insight, clarity and connection.

Throughout 2017, members have been hard at work submitting, critiquing and re-submitting work for our second publication Orange. If you have read Red, you will know the writers are expected to place a piece of orange in every tale, no matter which genre. We hope you enjoy these diverse, provocative and often humorous tales.

Carol Salter
Founder & Chair
Inspirations Writers Group

https://inspirationswritersgroup.weebly.com/

A Grave Error

by Tricia Brady

Bert's wife Vera nagged, bullied and tormented him constantly, making his life a misery.

After work, Bert met his mates in his local pub, The Last Chance. This was Bert's only refuge, a chance to talk over a few pints, before going home after a hard day's graft digging graves. After chatting about the usual things like work, sport and politics, they were relaxed enough for Bert to talk about the problems with his wife.

"She's driving me mad with her pernickety ways," Bert moaned.

"I wouldn't stand for it," said Loony Len, as he supped his beer. "My wife takes orders from me – except on Saturdays." Bert wanted to ask why not Saturdays, but thought better of it.

"Stand up for yourself!" shouted Deaf Duke, as he downed yet another pint.

"For goodness sake Bert, are you a man or a mouse?" whispered Silent Sam, getting up to use the Gents.

Their advice continued like this for an hour or so, then they made their excuses to leave. No one dared upset his own wife and be late home. They left Bert sitting in the pub thinking, until almost closing time. He had a plan, but would he be brave enough to carry it out? As he left the pub Bert looked up at the pub sign, lit a cigarette and decided, *It's an omen. I'll do it tonight.*

Bert knew there was only one burial the following day because he'd dug the grave, and he knew that no relatives or friends would be present either – it would be a pauper's funeral.

When Bert got home he climbed the stairs, careful not to tread on the squeaky step. Hearing snores and grunting sounds coming from the spare bedroom, he entered. Vera usually occupied the main bedroom and he slept in the spare room. Sometimes, just to be annoying, she would swap rooms like she'd done tonight. It didn't worry Bert where she slept as long as it wasn't with him.

As he opened the door a faint orange light from the streetlight shone into the room, just enough for him to see the pillow which had fallen to the floor. He picked it up and using all his strength, held it firmly over Vera's face until he felt no resistance. Bert placed her dead body in a large plastic bag which he'd pilfered from work and kept in the boot of his car together with his tools, a spade and ladder. It had never occurred to him they'd be used for the murder of his wife.

With the body in the boot, he drove back to the cemetery. Bert knew the exact position of the newly dug grave. He removed the orange tarpaulin, placed the ladder in the hole, stepped down and started digging again. When he thought it was deep enough, he lowered Vera's body down and covered it with soil. Tomorrow's coffin would be placed on top and no one would know Vera was underneath. Of course, he'd have to feign sadness and practice being distraught when it was discovered his wife had left him.

Arriving home later, exhausted, Bert purposely stepped on the squeaky step, continued up the stairs and flopped into bed still wearing his work clothes. The thought of Vera shouting at him for doing just that, and not having had a shower, made him grin. Now, he could do as he pleased. He'd never have to answer to her again.

Bert, was about to fall asleep when he heard the toilet flush. He sat bolt upright as the bedroom door opened. He was horrified to see his wife standing there.

"Bert, where have you been?" Vera snapped, as she switched on the light. "Why are you so late?" she said, her voice rising in anger. "What's the matter with you? You look like you've seen a ghost. And, why are you still wearing those disgusting clothes? You know how much I hate them! Change them at once and have a shower, you stink!"

As she got into bed she muttered, "Oh! I forgot to tell you, my sister's staying with us - she's sleeping in the spare room."

ATHENA'S ODYSSEY

BY NIKI SAKKA

Invaders brought a political tsunami to Athena's homeland. They spread death and misery to thousands of people. They demolished the outcome of years of hard work and destroyed so many beautiful dreams.

The new political situation throughout the entire country erased the chance of a perfect future for Athena and her parents. It separated her from her family. It forced her to move far from home. The last moments at home were like a painful scene from a nightmare for the whole family. Despite that, those moments had become a precious memory for Athena and would always hold a permanent place in her heart of hearts.

Rebecca, her mother, fastened a gold cross on a chain around Athena's neck and said, "It's from the Holy Land, to keep you safe." Then, wrapping her arms around her, squeezing her close to her chest, she kissed her on both cheeks. Hot tears were streaming down both their necks.

Michael, her father, had tried to control his emotions. "You are a strong, sensible girl. Have faith and everything will be okay," he said, his voice shaking. He gave Athena a warm hug and kissed her a final goodbye. Athena felt his heart pumping against the skinny bones of his chest.

It wasn't the first time Athena had lived away from home, but that had been under completely different circumstances. Now, she didn't have the security and the support her parents provided for her. Many changes were happening in her life, most of them completely out of her control.

The fact that she had to leave the place called home, with the possibility that she would never be allowed to step foot on that soil again, was too hard for her to accept. Her parents, and people close to her, remained in the war zone under military law. Athena wasn't even allowed to write a letter to them. The only way to stay in touch was to use the Red Cross 'Open Message' forms. The thought that she was unlikely to see her parents in person again and, above all, what the separation was probably doing to them, was killing her.

As a refugee, Athena moved to a free, democratic country where she had human and legal rights, like any other immigrant citizen. However, she had to live among strangers and in unknown places. She had to face unforeseeable challenges for her survival.

That was a new beginning for her.

The beginning of her 'Odyssey!'

She was a young and newly-qualified primary school teacher. As soon as she moved there, she went to the education office to apply for a teaching job. There were hundreds of other applicants. A member of staff suggested, "If you want my advice, instead of wasting your money buying a stamp for the application form, go and buy a lottery ticket. You've got more chance of winning that than getting a job!" That sounded a bit harsh but was not far from the truth. The number of applicants was much higher than the number of vacant posts.

Athena's good grades helped her to get a one-year contract at a school in a beautiful holiday resort. Her colleagues, the parents and villagers, were friendly and hospitable, beyond her expectation. They provided the help and moral support she desperately needed.

The teaching, and the time she spent with her new acquaintances, killed the daytime. Getting through the night alone was complete agony. From the moment when she opened the outside door and went into the empty, silent flat, the anguish overwhelmed her. Her heart started to pump faster. Her memories grew, and within seconds had overpowered her rational thinking and her feelings. It was like everything around her came to life with a monstrous face. But as soon as she switched the radio on, she started feeling a bit calmer. She still felt unease, but it was more manageable. Athena had expected to feel a bit disorientated, but not to that degree. Every night she kept the radio and the lights on to relax and sleep.

The following year Athena had to move to a different school, to another unfamiliar place, in a little mountainside village. She rented the only available living accommodation. It was a small, detached bungalow, surrounded by a garden full of overgrown rose bushes, jasmine, geraniums, bougainvillea and other colourful blooms.

Although it was in the middle of a good neighbourhood, she would never have moved there if she had had a choice. She didn't like to travel long distances, and most of all, she didn't want this disgraceful feeling – this *phobia* – to dominate her life.

I can do it, I can beat it. Athena promised herself.

On the first day in the new house, Athena's best friends, Anna and Maria, came to help her settle in. They were busy unpacking, when a knock on the door brought an unexpected visitor. A slim, middle-aged lady, dressed in black. Her black headscarf revealed just the two big, turquoise-green eyes, pointed nose and thin, pale lips.

"Welcome, dear! I brought you some figs and a cake. I've just made it. It's still warm, your favourite," she said with a broad smile, and a very sweet welcoming voice.

Athena was shocked and surprised! She just managed to say, "Thank you, it's very kind of you …" The lady squeezed Athena's hand with affection and left.

"*Your* favourite? What is all that about?" Maria asked.

"I don't know… and the way she squeezed my hand like we knew each other …" Athena said, with some wonderment.

"Do you think she is some sort of sorceress? I mean, like a fortune-teller? It's an orange cake, your favourite one, and figs, your favourite fruit. How could she possibly know that?" Anna exclaimed.

"There is definitely something strange about that lady, no doubt about it," Athena said.

"Oh, definitely – but the cake is delicious – yum!" Maria mumbled, through a mouthful. They all laughed and enjoyed a slice.

A few months later, Athena was marking papers one night, when she heard a neighbour woman scream, "I saw him! I saw him! I'm telling you! He is here!"

"It was just a shadow, for goodness sake," a male voice said in an annoyed tone.

"No! No, it's my boy! He is back!" her cries disturbed the night's peaceful silence.

Athena looked out through the window. She realised that it was Dorothy Roussos, the lady who had brought the cake and figs, who was screaming.

Eventually a complete silence veiled the whole area.

The next morning, she asked her landlord, who lived close by, about the previous night.

"Oh, forget it. Ignore Dorothy. Just avoid her," he said.

On her way to school Athena saw Dorothy coming up the road towards her. She was scowling, holding something flat and square-shaped, like a picture, shielding her chest. Athena thought this was a chance to find out what had happened the night before, and straight from the horse's mouth. However, before Athena had a chance to say anything, Dorothy slowed her pace, looking at Athena as she passed her. "I saw Jimmy. My boy visited you," she told her. "I'm not mad," she added then walked away briskly.

What did she mean by that? Athena wondered, feeling more confused than ever. There was absolutely no rational explanation for Dorothy's behaviour.

In springtime, Anna and Maria visited Athena again. The sun was shining, so they decided to go for a walk. They wanted to explore the other side of the nearby woods, up the hill. The view was breath-taking. In a nice spot, there was a wooden bench with a golden plaque which read:

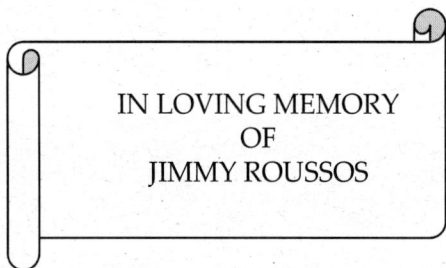

IN LOVING MEMORY
OF
JIMMY ROUSSOS

They sat there enjoying the magnificent setting, breathing in the fresh breeze from the conifer trees. The pleasant scent of wild flowers was everywhere, and the colours turned the scene into a brilliant tapestry.

Late afternoon they returned home. When Athena's friends left she went to bed. She thought about the bench in the woods. From

with itself. I always thought having one's portrait painted such narcissism. The strange thing is, I have always hated my photograph taken. I never looked quite how I thought I did. The camera never lies! How true indeed. Perhaps he will be kind to me? Maybe if I hold my head a little higher, tilt my chin upwards, suck in my cheeks?

She's at it again. Not only can't she sit still, but now she starts to change her pose. Oh, what the heck – give them what they want. It's no skin off your nose if you make your paintings half-truths. Well, big fat lies, actually. A little darker flesh tones here to shorten her nose; lighten it a shade under the eyes; some russet strokes to create hollows and narrow the face; some rosy tones to create the desired high cheek bones. Yes, just right.

My stomach's tightening – it looks like he's finishing off. Oh, please God, let me not be disappointed, or worse, embarrassed. Why, it's rather good. No, it's not good – it's lovely! Do I really look like that? Don't giggle like that, you silly woman, and take that inane smile off your face – he will think you vain. Just wait until I put that on the wall at home. It will make the girls envious. Now, what sort of frame would suit it I wonder?

Oh yes, just as I thought. She likes it. Of course, she likes it – you've made her look a million dollars. She won't worry about a facelift now – she has physical proof of her beauty. I expect she is already thinking about the frame to choose to go with the colour schemes. Sad really that all my hard work and talent is reduced to whether or not it complements the lounge curtains. Ah well, matters not – here comes the cash!

CONTEMPLATIONS

BY ERNESTINA FETISSOVA

Inhabited in small
events
the everyday
unfolds

Talking to neighbours
walking the dog
drifting in human
narrative . . .

Today
south-westerly wind brings
lightness to walking
joys of verbality

In mirror reflection
patina of time
looks back
at me

Nuggets of thoughts
floating
like ice on the river
in spring

Remains of the autumn
rain falls
on tired greenery
at dusk

seaside trip
girl runs along the beach . . .
this simple scenery in front
not meant to be for me

Sliver of the fading moon
birds silent fly
so many times described
but still exalts
translucent image lingers
for awhile
then stream of thoughts
takes over

windy night
swinging halo of street lamps
conjuring forms
and plays with meanings

befriend your demons
as easy life
obsessed but with
banalities

these days
birds waking up long
after me

sunsets sunrises
start framing days
far too fast

reading preface
reading postscript
glimpsing at life in between

on the altar
withered plastic bag
once brightly coloured
was placed

my house
full of numinous things
they do not speak
vernacular

tai chi in the garden
passing cat freezes
with eyes opened
wildly

old folks' tales
wearing new-born into submission
to dullness of life

do you remember orange people
and orange book for exercise
all this had passed
ecstatics dissipated like phantom wave
ooshshshooo . . .
thank you bagwan for glimpse
inside divine sat-chit-ananda

DEAR 110 MILKWOOD ROAD

BY VALERIE TYLER

Dear 110 Milkwood Road,
    I wonder where you are and if you remember me. It's only by
small chance that you'll receive this letter as I know not of your
whereabouts. I'm fully aware that you've been taken, because the
last time I went back to visit you, your brick built body lay
demolished on the ground, unrecognisable, leaving only a memory
of your spirit to confide in.

Silent atmosphere of emptiness shrouded the area. I looked for you, and realised the empty space before me in the heart of Brixton was where you'd stood.

My mind searched the rubble looking for memories. I found plenty there. Suddenly there you were again like you always had been, the welcoming brown door in front of me was ajar and I slowly walked in. The hallway seemed to loom. I'd always thought it was too dark with its brown and green paint. The lino, mimicking parquet flooring, was curled up with wear in places, revealing wooden floorboards underneath. I walked past the large bay-windowed living room and saw Uncle Eric putting newspaper around the fireguard to make the fire draw, waiting for orange flames to come alive, turning the room into the sacral belly of the house, a place for everyone to gather and share their creativity. On the arms of the brown leather couch a newspaper was open to the horse racing page. He liked a bet. The bedroom where my parents and I slept had wooden sliding doors that divided it from the main living room. It opened onto a small back yard, bordered by a high brick wall with the railway behind. On down the hall. On the right, I saw the larder where Nan Martha kept food supplies, jars of jams, pickles, and all sorts. To the left, a door leading to the back yard, known as a tradesmen's entrance in some houses.

Looking straight ahead and taking hold of the polished brass handle, I hesitantly entered the kitchen. It was full of activity. I saw Nan Martha bending down taking roast potatoes from the old black range, using her flowery apron for an oven glove. No health and safety in those days. She looked up, smiling, rosy cheeks blushed with heat. The copper kettle on the top of the range whistled its head off literally, water spouting everywhere.

Uncle Charlie polished his shoes. The shoe grooming kit was kept on a shelf behind a curtain. If it had been a Friday he'd have been picking cockles from their shells with a pin. The wooden table was covered with a plastic table cloth proudly wiped to match the cleanliness of the daily-scrubbed floor. It was hard work in those days. Nan was often on her knees, scrubbing. The massive step through to the scullery where the sink was had caused a few accidents. Once, I'd cut my lip open, falling down it. My cousin Dave had got the blame. I remembered feeling awful as I'm sure he

17

didn't mean to push me. There were at least five of us children in that house at the same time which probably didn't seem too daunting for Nan Martha, as she'd had ten.

The grandad chair was still there. I sat in that many a time. The only advantage of being a girl was that I was allowed to sit in it. "Only my little farthing-face can sit here," Grandad used to say. The boys were more spoilt by Uncle Eric, who loved being back in a boy's world, and saw any excuse to indulge them with what he probably never had as a child.

My cousins and I tried hard to keep out of everyone's way; we didn't mind the overcrowding which was frowned upon by the adults. Kevin and I used to sit under the table with Gyp the dog. We'd pretend we were a family of bears making honey and I knew that one day I would marry him. Of course, I came to realise that wasn't possible, just in case you're wondering.

In bed, I'd listen to the train carriages banging together on the tracks. I loved the sound. It was what I knew of the railway. I wasn't allowed to sit on the wall with my cousins and watch the trains out back, or play with the go kart out front. A boy's life seemed more exciting.

When I left you, I'm not sure if I said goodbye. I was only three, but of course I did come back many times after that. I recall screaming uncontrollably at the threshold of our new flat. Being in a beautiful place near Wimbledon Common didn't compensate for leaving my cousins behind. I had thought they'd join us later but they never did. I came to see more of my cousin Maureen who lived in Essex. We became very good friends and still are.

When we came back we occasionally stayed the night in my Aunt Rose and Uncle Jim's room with Kevin and Michael. Gary came along a few years after that. It was a dimly lit room and I had to sleep in a cot. My cousins Pat and Dave lived upstairs and my two uncles shared a room. Many of us lived under your roof. Happy times were had in there, full of laughter and an occasional argument. We were not allowed to swear or answer back. I learnt the art of manners and gratitude at a young age.

As I turned to leave you, I heard a mouth organ playing and saw Grandad George Tamaline sitting by the fire which was now glowing orange. His fingers danced over the mouth organ and my dad accompanied him. They stamped their feet to music that gradually mellowed from 'If you ever go to Ireland' to 'Three coins in a fountain.'

I was told that around the corner and not too far away David Bowie was born. I think I left Brixton at about the same time as he did.

Even though you may no longer be physically accessible or seen through other's eyes, memories will linger in the ether, and form stories of nostalgia in the rooms of my mind. You were a world unto your own, so to me you still and always will exist. To me you had an orange heart, one that filled me with a burning sacral desire to share with others the love you taught, for how else would they know love if they hadn't met you?

You taught me that love is not only accessible through comfort, easy living and pampering, but sits waiting to be found in cold walls and dark spaces, whether you're rich or poor, young or old. You were my first love and I, so young, was nurtured and moulded in your strong, steadfast walls.

Yours Sincerely.

Valerie. x

EVASION

BY LEE RUSSELL

I've done a lot of hard things for Queen and Country. How much luck can one man have? How long before I pay the price?

I hate myself for loving this excitement, the chase, living in the moment.

They knew the right strings to pull to get me out here. I leapt for it like a salmon rushing to spawn, desperate to prove that I've still got it, like I was still young, still virile. Desperate to avoid the shame of losing four agents in Russia. They twisted me around that shame, like I've done so many times myself. Bloody Secret Intelligence Service; they filled my ears with all the denials that I was already deceiving my conscience with: 'There's no fault in it for you, Alec. Nobody could have known how they'd react.'

Well I SHOULD have known! That's my job! Now the whole team is dead because of me. Three years' work up in smoke and nothing to show for it except for four corpses. But those four corpses did manage to get Jakub Novak's film canister all the way from Novaya Zemlya, each passing it on just before they were killed. And now it's in my hands.

I hate them for getting me to do this. No, I'm lying to myself. I knew what they were doing.

'We trust you to get this done, Alec,' they said. They trust me, how much I wanted to hear that! But if I fail . . . if I'm captured . . . what then? Nothing. They will deny knowing anything about me, and I will be corpse number five.

That other one was getting too close. I can still see his face, shocked as the knife went in . . . NO! Stop it! Stop snivelling and pick yourself up! Nothing is more important than the defence of the realm. This is what you signed up for. This is who you are. Deal with it!

They won't have found him yet. Just got to keep calm. Keep alert.

Alert? That's a joke. Forty hours awake . . . God, I'm so tired. They'd better be ready. This is going to end soon.

Need to keep moving, leaving enough false leads so they confuse the real contact for just another detour.

I hate this city. Cold, grey, dusty, dirty. Full of dusty, dirty people with miserable faces and lifeless eyes. I feel them looking at me, examining, constantly checking if I belong. I don't make eye contact, just keep moving, obeying the social rules, blending in.

My clothes are bland: worn black sports jacket over a dark grey t-shirt, blue jeans, worn grey trainers. No logos. No bright colours. No hat. No sunglasses. No bag. Dusty face, but not dirty. Nothing to make them remember me as I walk past.

There's the department store entrance. Time to make them work a bit more! I almost walk past and then duck inside at the last moment. Moving fluidly, I cross the floor quickly, picking up a security-tagged perfume box, weaving between shoppers without attracting their attention. There's the back exit onto the street, just past the staircase leading to the lower ground-floor. I toss the box through the anti-theft sensors by the door and immediately bound down the steps as the alarm sounds behind me. The chase is on!

Ninety seconds to cross the lower floor and reach the staircase leading back to the main entrance. I take a moment to compliment the lady running the perfume counter as I leave. They'll see that and have to pull her in for questioning. It'll be fast and rough on her but I can't think about that now.

I'm usually one step ahead, knowing I'm going to outpace them. This time it feels different. Death is behind me . . . don't look around! I feel it chasing my heels, seeking the right moment.

I can't keep this up much longer.

I take a few deeper breaths, exhaling slowly, face neutral throughout. Breathe in, and out, in, and out. Relax. While you're breathing you're alive.

My nose has an itch like the dirt from a million people has been squeezed into it. Ignore it. Keep your hands down!

The steady roar of traffic, the chatter and clatter from thousands of people forcing their way past each other overwhelms my hearing. If they come quietly I won't hear them. But I don't think they'll do it in such a public place.

I walk at the crowd's pace, careful not to encroach on the people in front or hinder those following. I keep close to the store fronts, staying away from the kerb where I could be pushed into traffic.

Blue lights flash at the end of the street. They won't be for me; I'd be taken down long before I saw a road block.

Three men in suits turn the corner ahead, causing a wave of movement as people close up to let them pass. Two are walking side by side, one following. The one behind sips from a take-away coffee cup but otherwise their hands are empty. Their grey jackets flap over crisp white shirts as they walk, no sign of concealed guns. I make glancing eye-contact with the closest man as he gets within three feet of me. He looks away without interest, acknowledging my presence as an obstacle without acknowledging me as a human being; true city style. No threat.

Without breaking my stride, I drop an empty sandwich wrapper into a bin as I walk past. I smile slightly; they'll enjoy searching that!

A loud metallic squeal on my right. I keep walking ahead but my eyes flick to look across the road to where a grimy refuse lorry is lowering its hydraulic tailgate. Just one man in stained overalls is standing at the back, working the controls, concentrating on what he's doing. No threat.

I reach the corner and follow it around rather than attempting to cross the road junction. The smell of exhaust is strong here, where vehicles are sitting, waiting for the traffic lights to change. People are clustered by the pedestrian crossings, all facing the road, nobody looking towards me. No threat. For a second I stand in the crowd and move my hands near a young man's rucksack before moving on. People nearby will have seen me simply massage my hands for a moment, but from behind it will look like I pushed something in.

The sky abruptly darkens as a cloud moves overhead, grey and heavy, full of anticipation of rain. A light wind rises, lifting city grime into the air. I squint to keep my eyes clear from the tiny gritty particles.

As I walk I watch the reflections of the people behind me in the shop windows. He's still there, I'm sure of it. He stays just a little too far away for me to see him directly, but I know he is back there, following, watching. He disturbs the rhythm of the people around him and their body language betrays his presence.

It's a struggle to keep my situational awareness this high.

He's been there for at least an hour. He must know that I've guessed he's there. So why does he stay back?

They can't be sure if I've made the drop off, or it's still to come. That must be it; they suspect, but they're not sure. So they're playing me. The hook is in but they hope I can't feel the tug of the line yet.

The crowd is carrying me towards a stall on the next corner. There is no avoiding this moment, it has to be now. If I pass by, when I return, they'll know.

I can smell the fruit he is selling from a few feet away. Small punnets of strawberries are stacked in a pyramid at the front of his display, blood red, glistening, enticing. There is a steady stream of people stopping for a moment to buy some and enjoy his patter.

"Lovely day . . . beautiful strawbs these, straight from the field into the market this morning . . ."

"Three punnets? Yes, sir, I can bag them for you . . ."

"Feels like rain, but that might be nice for a change, eh?"

He looks the part. Tanned, worn skin on a wrinkled face. Strong hands with fingers as thick as sausages, nails as tough as iron. A plainly coloured fleece jacket, which might have been bright blue once, but is now a grey, city blue.

I step forward and he looks at me enquiringly: "What's for you, guv?"

"Lovely strawberries," I say, nodding at them. "But what I'd really like is an orange. Do you have one?"

His laughing eyes harden at my words. "They're not really in season yet, mate. But I got a few this morning. Sold the first box and haven't had time to put the other lot out," he says.

"Strawberries give a quick rush of flavour but it goes away quickly. Orange stays with you for ages," I say.

He nods slightly. "Yes, that's very true," he says. "Just the one?"

"Yes, please."

"Bagged? Or are you eating it now?"

"I'll eat it just down the road, by the river. But I'd find a bag helpful, if you don't mind?"

"Sure, mate." He bends down behind the stall for a moment. When he stands back up he holds out a brown paper bag at arms' length, which he deftly flicks to wrap around the orange. "Eighty cents, please," he says.

I take the bag and palm the small canister to him as I hand over a note: "Keep the change," I tell him. He's already selling the next punnet as I walk away.

I re-join the flow and move towards the old docks area. The crowd starts to thin out as the buildings change from shiny urban regenerations, all bright glass and chrome, to crumbling industrial facades. The closer I get to the waterside the more decayed the buildings around me become, as if the river itself is slowly pulling them down, erasing man's footsteps from its shores.

A man is sitting on a sleeping bag in the doorway of a boarded-up ruin. I bend over and toss a few coins into his pot. "Thanks, man," he says. He won't be thanking me in a minute.

I emerge from the old city quarters onto an open wharf that, for a single moment, feels unnaturally exposed. I imagine pairs of eyes hiding in the shadows of the nearby buildings, watching me.

I see the old mooring bollard by the waterside, coated with rust, spattered with bird droppings. I walk over, sit down and start to peel the orange while I watch the water flow beneath my feet. It is alive, whirling and swirling, watching me, waiting to be fed.

At least I don't have it any more. All I have to do is play the last act of the game. Throw them off the scent. Keep them guessing.

My backup team will have been organising the pickup as soon as I gave the code phrase. There should be a three-minute wait from the moment I sat down here. 'You make your own luck with thorough preparation,' my Controller taught me. In the last stage of the game it always comes down to that; who has the most knowledge, who is better prepared, who will have the most luck.

I hear his footsteps approaching but don't turn around. Three minutes.

"A moment of your time, Mr Hendy," he says. "If you would be so good as to come with me? No fuss. Make it easy for yourself."

"You know me?" I ask him in reply.

"We know everything, Mr Hendy. You've taken us on quite a tour today. There didn't seem to be a pattern to your movements at first. You wanted us to think you were randomly wandering, like a tourist. But your subconscious let you down. Like any hunted animal you were drawn toward the places you felt safe, the places you know best, where you have stayed in safe houses."

"Safe houses? What are you talking about?" I keep my back turned towards him, that's important. Stretch the time, make him wait.

"You've been here many times before, Mr Hendy. We know where you stayed and how long for. We know who you saw, what you said, what you ate, everything."

"That's a lot of fuss for tracking a tourist," I reply.

"No need to keep up the pretence. You were photographed receiving the film canister containing the stolen data about the

24

prototype ballistic missile. We have followed that canister closely, keeping up the pressure and pulling in everyone involved in the chain to smuggle it out. That chain ends here with you, Mr Hendy."

.I sit quietly for a moment, letting the clock tick.

Ninety seconds.

Turning around on the bollard to face him, I continue to peel the orange and then slip a segment into my mouth, delicious.

"I think you're confusing me with someone else," I say. "I don't know anything about canisters or Novaya Zemlya."

He pulls a gun from his pocket. "I know you are unarmed. You have been scanned many times as you moved around our city."

That was the point of walking past some of those scanners. I smile inside but keep my face expressionless.

"You can come with me now, and we will search you in the privacy of a cell. Or I can shoot you here and search your body in the rain. Your choice." He smiles. He thinks he has me.

I hear the diesel engine of a boat turning the corner as it pulls in towards the wharf.

"You've thought of everything," I tell him with a resigned expression on my face.

"Yes, we have."

There is a single loud gunshot and he falls backwards onto the ground.

I get up and stand over his body. Blood flowing from the exit wound is collecting into a vivid red puddle around him. His face looks surprised. His open eyes seem to be imploring for this not to be true.

I should feel sorry for him, but I don't. I don't feel anything anymore. We're both tools. Both used by our masters to achieve their goals. This time I won. *One point for the away-team!* Careful now – I'm being too cynical. That sense of having no emotion comes just before it all floods out, and that can't happen here!

Above me the clouds finally burst and cold rain quickly plasters my clothes to my body. Looking down I see his blood washing from the cobbles into the water. The river is erasing yet another mark from its banks.

The boat is waiting. It's about thirty feet long, with a small cabin in front of hard bench-seating beneath a canvas awning.

The shooter drops down from the cabin roof and disappears inside. I climb down the ladder, hop over the gunwale and follow him in.

There are two of them in the cabin. One is wearing a snagged captain's hat and has his hands on the wheel. The other, with fair tussled hair, is putting the rifle into a hidden compartment under the radio console.

"Nice shot," I say. "Bang on time. Where are we heading?"

"Up river, into the estuary. We'll blend into the normal traffic. This boat is not suspected. We shouldn't be stopped," the captain says. He moves the boat out, drifting into the main current, following the flow towards the sea.

I see a metal cash box on top of a bundle of river tour leaflets by the window. I pull out a fifty euro note and drop it in.

"There's no charge for this trip!" the captain laughs.

"We all pay the ferryman somehow. I prefer cash in this life, lest he decides to ask for something else," I reply.

The captain thinks for a moment before replying. "Might be something in that," he says eventually.

I sit on the side as the boat chugs on up river, watching the dark, inky water as it flows around the bow and folds closed behind the stern, leaving just a few bubbles in our wake. Like we were never here.

FEVER

BY ANNE SIKORA LORD

The relentless antipodean sun had made the temperature unbearable in the roof space of the old Queenslander style homestead. It was so unlike her own chilly English attic. Long, sloping, rusted corrugated iron roofing efficiently caught whatever rain fell in the 'wet'. A wrap-around veranda did its best to keep the inner sanctum cool in the 'dry'. Within the shadowy loft, it felt like a long hot night, as Rebecca sifted through the detritus of the remains of her inheritance in the gloomy atmosphere. Small slivers of light penetrated cracks, barely supplemented by a sole light bulb which flickered each time the generator in the shed kicked into action. Sheep bleated plaintively in the distance.

Her attention was drawn to a crooked stack of books perched on top of a battered trunk. She impatiently brushed off the dusty years of history that had settled on the covers. As she separated them, clean areas between revealed unexciting titles; 'Sheep Husbandry', and 'Growing Cereals in Adverse Climates'. But one captured her interest. A green mould-spotted leather cover was embossed in gold with 'Nursing Journal'. It must have been someone with money, Rebecca considered, as she opened the book. A photograph fell from between the pages, fluttering to the splintered wooden floorboards, along with a yellowing piece of paper.

The photograph, devoid of colour, revealed a row of people standing outside a group of canvas tents. Four women and two men, not all obligingly looking in the direction of the camera, but one woman, no more than a young girl stared out defiantly, her chin jutting forward, a serious look on her face. She was wearing what appeared to be a nurse's uniform – a full-length plain dress with a high collar, a long, white apron starched to within an inch of its life, and an equally stiff headdress resembling a nun's veil. The other three women also wore aprons but their general dress was scruffy. The two men both sported full beards and wire-framed spectacles, their long-jacketed suits giving them an air of importance. Who were these people? Rebecca flipped the photograph, her question answered in tiny inky notations –

'Left to right ~ Dr. McIllroy (an unfortunate name considering he is expected to cure the sick); Dr. O'Brian (a sweet man and so good with the children); Lillian (nursing aid and my best friend); Sissy (orderly); Bea (cook); me (looking like a cross-patch).'

Rebecca turned her attention from the photograph to the paper, unfolding it with care as it had fragmented in parts along the creases. Smoothing it out, revealing its aged orange margins, she rested it on the surface of the journal.

"Qualities of the Virtuous Nurse" she read out loud, and scanned the alphabetical lists of words. Some jumped out at her – 'Absolute loyalty (to doctors); gentle demeanour; quietness; prudence; silence (particularly 'controlled tongues'); altruism; charity; chastity; obedience,' the list went on.

She laughed at some – 'abstinence (from drugs, alcohol and sex); cleanliness (morally and physically); and pleasing, attractive manners'.

God! she thought, *Who wrote this? It must have been a man!* She looked back at the men in the photo and it started to make sense. Her Aunt Esme had been a nurse in the First World War. Great-Great Aunt Esme, to be exact. Could this be her? She looked at the uniformed figure and examined her face for similarities to her own. The photo was not only sepia, but slightly out of focus, which made it hard to distinguish features. She convinced herself that the almond eyes staring at her, mirrored her own.

She couldn't help herself reading the rest of the list – 'compassion; compliance (with authority); conscientiousness; self-sacrifice; endurance; spirit of service to humanity; ending with womanliness.' *Huh! Wouldn't see many of those on the list of nursing qualities today,* she laughed to herself, reflecting on her own hard-earned medical degree and occasional struggle, even in these days, to be accepted as an equal to the men.

She placed the photo and paper to one side, and opened the journal. Its spine creaked as the delicate pages separated to a red ribbon bookmark, its tail a faded orange where it had been exposed to light. She began to read the opening sentences, written in a precise but flowing script.

'Karragooree Hospital, Western Australia
12th May 1895

'As I write the date, the irony hits me; it is the birthday of the wonderful Florence Nightingale. I remembered it because she became my heroine during my training in London, and here I am in the middle of nowhere trying to follow her teachings. Kalgoorlie is a day's journey if we need supplies, and the Gold Rush has released another kind of fever into the desert. Typhoid!

'The lack of water here and unhygienic conditions make it such a struggle to cope. Coupled with the inadequate disposal of waste, newly

arrived settlers quickly succumb to the disease. It is the children I worry about – they will be lucky to see five years of age. These people come with hopes of finding their fortune, some having never held a pick before, let alone dug a mine. They soon realise the desperate situation they have brought their families to. The cost of gold in human lives cannot be measured.

'Our so-called hospital is nothing more than a group of hessian tents, no different to those of the miners. There is nothing but red earth as far as the eye can see, under a vast unforgiving cerulean sky. How I miss the gentle ultramarine of the English firmament. Even the few trees here are a subdued grey-green. The dust penetrates even the most hidden away of crevices.

'I have to remain reserved and cannot let them see my innermost feelings. I confess to crying myself to sleep each night.'

Rebecca stopped reading. *How horrendous it all sounds*, she thought, contrasting it with how she had come here, over a century later, to work in paediatrics at the modern Perth General. Curiosity aroused, she opened the book to another random entry.

'Karragooree Hospital

21st December 1895

'Christmas is soon upon us, not that it will make any difference to my patients. Many are so taken by the fever they are barely conscious or at the very least troubled by delusions. The heat and the mosquitos are burdensome. I have strung up some muslin around my own bed to protect myself, but during the day there is no way to avoid being bitten.'

Again, Rebecca paused. It was a door to another world. How did they endure such conditions? She was about to turn to another page when her phone bleeped, reminding her to get a move on. Late shift was due to start in an hour, and it took at least forty-five minutes to get into the city. She couldn't complain – it would have been two days by horse and cart for Esme. Repositioning the bookmark, Rebecca reluctantly closed the journal. Tucking it under her arm she flicked off the light, closed off the hatch, and descended the ladder. Grabbing her bag, slamming the front door and still grasping the journal, she made her way out to her Land Cruiser.

* * *

The afternoon had been busy on the children's ward. Rebecca expected this with the soaring summer temperature. Sunburn, play accidents, a partial drowning, the usual suspects had all demanded her attention – everyone went a little crazy in the heat. She had been treating sunstroke in Zack, a little boy no more than a toddler, who had a history of epilepsy so was being closely monitored by the nursing staff. She had popped in and out to check on him between the never-ending stream of other cases.

At the first opportunity to take a break Rebecca went to her locker and retrieved her Aunt's journal from her rucksack, determined to read more. She collapsed into an armchair in the empty staffroom, toed off her 'Crocs', folded her legs beneath her and, locating the ribbon marker, continued to read.

'25*th* December 1895

'I was awoken just before midnight. The cries startled me. I had left the child whimpering on the little canvas cot a few hours earlier, but the mewing had turned to a full-blown scream. With my eyes still adjusting to the darkness, I had crashed into Lillian's bed as I passed, disturbing her sleep. I felt my way to the tent entrance and lit my oil lamp before heading to the main hospital building. No longer a tent, but the makeshift wooden building, with its corrugated metal roof, is still a long way from perfect. My lamp had been inadequate, but I fumbled along the familiar rows of beds in haste to prevent the cries from waking the rest of the ward.

'The boy child had been named Bapp, meaning Blue Gum, by the aboriginal girls here. It was at the base of such a tree that he had been found abandoned.

'The child's dark skin was damp and hot, but he was shivering. I gently pinched a dent in his flesh but the lack of water in his body meant it failed to spring back. He had been lethargic all day, but by now had become sleepless and was sweating profusely. I attempted to cool his little body, but opening a window was not an option, and fanning him only swirled the warm air around him. I reached for the bowl of water at the side of Bapp's cot. It had become tepid in the night air. I bathed the child with wrung out cloths, but his temperature continued to rise. The fever was getting worse. His skin had become a blotchy red.

'I left him for a few minutes to find some cold water.'

Rebecca's mind wandered from the book. Her own training had made her aware that the rise in temperature with fever was one of the ways our immune system attempts to combat infection. Would Esme have known this? Did she even have a thermometer? Rebecca resumed her reading.

'On my return to the child's bedside I soon saw that he had deteriorated. Irritability had turned to delirium. His confused look as his eyes tried to focus on my face, accompanied by the briefest smile as he recognised me, broke my heart. He had no-one but me to comfort him, belonged to no-one but the land. Rape of the gins (as young females are called, a shortened colloquial form of 'aborigine', a term I deplore), has become a regular feature of this unruly, godforsaken township (if you indeed could call it that!). It has left a growing number of unwanted children roaming the area, considered as neither black nor white, scrounging to survive.

'I sat for hours holding his hand and had drifted off on several occasions only to be woken by his distress. My limbs were stiff and I could not feel my feet, but I knew they were still there when the throbbing replaced numbness as my circulation returned. His temperature seemed to be rising rapidly, so I rose unsteadily and continued cooling him with the wet rags.'

"No!" shouted Rebecca, "It will make things worse – just leave him be." She felt foolish when she realised that she had said this aloud. *If only they had had the antipyretic drugs that are available today,* she thought. *It's easier these days, with twenty-first century medicine, and practice backed by research. Esme had it so hard.* Rushing on she turned the page, anticipating the inevitable.

'I prayed that it was typhoid and not the dreaded scarlet fever which had ravaged a neighbouring mine. I had read how it could result in kidney failure and certain death. Bapp then began to convulse.

'It was all too much. I reluctantly ignored my training. Obedience be damned! I picked him up!'

At that moment, the swing doors of the staffroom flew open, hitting the walls behind, breaking Rebecca's concentration.

"Doctor Lane. Doctor Lane!" a female voice called, "You're needed urgently – Zack is fitting."

She sprang to her feet, slipping back into her 'Crocs', she raced to the ward.

* * *

Several hours later, exhausted and dehydrated, Rebecca returned to the staffroom. Cardboard cup of coffee in hand, she gingerly sipped the steaming liquid.

Glancing at the sofa she realised Esme's journal was no longer where she had left it. Scanning the room in panic, Rebecca's hands shook, spilling the hot drink. Fatigue outweighing patience, she dumped the cup on a counter-top. Mopping her hands, her stained scrubs and the mess on the floor, she sighed heavily. Throwing the wet paper towels in the bin she spotted the mislaid journal on top of a pile of magazines. She snatched it up, resettled on the chair and resumed her reading.

'The heat transferred from his stiffening body to my arms as I tenderly held him and offered gentle reassurance, but he was too far gone to be aware. I could only wait until his tiny body returned to its flaccid state.

'As Christmas dawn broke to the sound of the throaty warble of the magpies, the seizures returned. Within minutes his little brown body had gone limp for the last time. I rocked his tiny form, more for my own self-comfort, as the tears escaped onto my cheeks. I kissed his head and tasted the saltiness of his drying sweat on my lips. I offered up a prayer for his soul. Where was this merciful God who would allow an innocent to die on Christ's birthday? I heard no answer other than the laugh of a nearby kookaburra.'

Rebecca closed the journal, almost religiously, and held it to her chest as her own tears fell unchecked.

Bapp? Zack? They could be interchangeable, one and the same, she thought, letting out a shuddering sigh. She knew she was tired, and the pressure and emotion of what had happened to Zack this afternoon contributed to upsetting her usual professional demeanour, but the tears were definitely for Bapp. What chance had he had?

A tentative knock on the doorframe, and a head peeped through.

"Sorry to bother you Doctor Lane, but we just wanted to say thank you for all you did for Zack today."

Two faces looked at her from across the room, their eyes red and swollen like her own. Zack's parents looked weary, all-in.

"Come in, come in!" Rebecca insisted, surreptitiously palming away the remaining tears, and stood to face them. They looked confused.

"Are you all right?" asked Wendy, concerned.

"I'm fine," she assured her, "just need some shut-eye." She went through Zack's after-care with them. "Bring him back if you are in any way worried, but he should be bouncing back in no time," Rebecca concluded.

Over a century had passed since Esme's administering and still children were vulnerable. Ironically, the team, at Rebecca's suggestion, had considered that Zack might have contracted scarlet fever. Global travel had caused the disease to rear its ugly head again after previous eradication. The tests came back negative. Lucky Zack, poor Bapp.

Finally, after she had made sure she had signed Zack's paperwork enabling him to leave the hospital, Rebecca returned to the staffroom. This time she chose the sofa, stretching out her aching limbs and doing a few shoulder shuffles to get comfortable. Propping her head on a couple of cushions, and resting the journal on her raised knees, she looked again at the gold-leafed title.

It wasn't just a journal; it charted a 'journey' from then to now. Although the language and practice was out-dated, the morals and ethics weren't. She would read more later; her eyes would not stay open for much longer. But she felt sure that Esme would have been proud of her today, and the feeling was mutual. A Great Aunt, a great lady.

FIRE FOX

BY SINEAD LE BLOND

There's a framed photo on the mantelpiece above the fireplace. It's you, peeking playfully through blades of grass. Visitors admire it.

"Oh, what a lovely picture! It's a red fox!" they exclaim.

Yes, I think, *It's a fox. But she's not an 'it', she's a vixen. And she's not just red.*

At least, not just 'red' to me.

In you, I see a flame, auburn, ablaze and tearing through the undergrowth, or amber, stretched along the sun-kissed shed roof.

I see cotton-wool white that spreads from pointed nose to soft belly. I see black velvet ears, front legs, and feet. I see the tip of your brush, black flecked with white.

Not 'just red'; a myriad of colours.

It's not their fault, these people. No, they say 'red' because they don't look properly. I don't challenge them. What's the point in getting into petty arguments, when all I want is for them to be astounded by your beauty?

It was on an indifferent day a year ago that I heard a rustling in the long grass at the back of my garden. I'd moved into this creaky old house with its unruly land a few months previously, with a plan. My heart had been broken and my ego dented when my ex-wife decided that her personal trainer was more of a man than me. I wanted to recover here, become self-sufficient. I envisaged growing my own food, chopping my own firewood. I wanted to reinvent my hum-drum self into someone I was proud to be. I was an IT consultant by profession, more comfortable with a hard drive than hard ground, but I was determined to succeed.

So far, living the 'Good Life' was proving to be a challenge. I was willing to be distracted from endless weeding. That tiny sound was enough for me to investigate. I thought there'd be a cat, or maybe a squirrel, foraging around. Nothing prepared me for the bright tawny eyes and quivering black nose that greeted me. Judging by the bewilderment in them, nothing had prepared you for encountering me either.

We stared at each other for a few seconds.

Then only a musky scent remained.

From that day, you surprised me constantly.

I'd gaze from an upstairs window, and glimpse a fiery streak whooshing through the undergrowth. I'd take the rubbish out, and a ginger bundle would be napping peacefully on the side path.

There you were, jumping a low wall. Here you were, playing on the lawn.

I wanted to make you welcome. I read up on what foxes liked to eat, and on their behaviour. I left honey sandwiches and raw chicken out each night. The land's wild spaces, hiding places, remained untouched.

Time in the garden became a shared experience. At first, you'd sit in the background, wary gaze fixed on me, ears twitching like radar. Over time, you crept a tiny bit closer to the action. I sensed that your curiosity matched mine.

I loved the summer evenings when a gentle breeze chased the heat out of the day. The setting sun cast soft pinks and golds across the lawn. I'd sit and ponder my day, and breathe in the delicate perfume of the wild flowers in the field beyond my land, spicy and sweet in the late warmth. Often, the long grass would swoosh, and you'd appear, glowing ochre in the half-light. You'd settle a 'flight distance' away, and gaze at me, head resting on your front paws.

And we talked. Well, I did all the talking, but you proved an attentive listener. I'd tell you about my plans for the house and the garden. You'd close your eyes in what seemed like approval when I spoke about keeping your hiding places, but a distinct frown crossed your face when I mentioned a water feature. If I chattered for too long, there'd be a stretch and yawn, a scratch behind an ear. I'm sure I saw a smile when I asserted that my DIY skills were improving.

You arrived on your terms, and you would retreat on them.

Summer slipped softly into autumn. The yellows, lilacs and sky blues of sunny days gave way to the deep greens, russets and browns of leaves turning. A smoky mist hung in the air.

I felt the first shivers of chill as I looked around, astounded about how much I'd achieved. Fruit canes had been planted, the beginnings of a vegetable and herb patch were emerging. There was a compost heap. An area near the field had been ear-marked for a mini orchard. I'd even arranged proper seating on the patio. As promised, your long grass remained untouched. I'd bowed to your greater judgment. There was no water feature in sight.

I glowed with pride. I was beginning to like myself again.

My new-found enjoyment of my home was marred only by your sudden absence. I knew foxes would disappear from time to time, and I took comfort in the fact that the food I left out each night vanished by morning.

On rare occasions, I glimpsed you sitting in the driving rain, your radiance muted. My heart ached.

The colourless weeks wore on. Eventually a watery winter sun appeared, promising new life in the weeks ahead.

One blustery Saturday morning in early March, I was wandering around the garden, planning spring projects. I stopped to look out across the field, and something caught my eye. Streaking towards me was a tiny orange comet. I stood, transfixed, as I watched it become you.

My joy turned to concern.

Something was wrong.

Your ears were flat against your head. The whites of your eyes stretched, stark, in your copper face. Your mouth was open, tongue lolling crazily out of one side. Exhausted, you kept running from some invisible danger. Your heartbeat was pulsing through your body. My heart was racing along with it.

You tore into the open shed and cowered in a corner, looking so small and scared. Why?

I heard it before I saw it. An atrocious cacophony of thundering hooves and braying hounds, bloodthirsty shouts and tuneless bugles, all underscored by the malevolent drone of quadbikes, rose out of nowhere. A split second later, they appeared in their sinister scarlet get-up. The local Hunt. No wonder you were terrified.

I'd heard about this mob.

Since the ban, they supposedly followed a trail, sniffed out by their hounds. Harmless enough, eh?

Locally, though, I'd heard tales of out-of-control packs of dogs chasing foxes into front gardens, cornering them and ripping them apart while members of the Hunt looked on. I'd heard about the thuggish behaviour of the "terrier men," the monsters who flushed out foxes from their earths for the Hunt to pursue. I'd heard how the riders would stand at the bar of the village pub and brag about their kills.

Now, here they were, apparently ready to bring all those grim tales to brutal life in their pursuit of you.

You were my friend, and they were trying to hurt you.

Rage propelled me forward. I jumped the ramshackle fence that divided the garden from the field. I paid no heed to hounds howling, horses roaring towards me, or voices warning me to get out of their way. I kept running to meet the oncoming crowd, screaming unintelligibly. Only when I was on the verge of entering the fray did my rational mind kick in.

I stopped, gasping.

Right.

It was just me, among a crowd armed with horses and hounds.

Fight or flight?

Well, I wasn't going anywhere.

A furious strength possessed me. I picked up whatever I could, and hurled it. Sticks, clumps of mud and rocks became airborne missiles. I hollered expletives. Had I been an onlooker, I'd have laughed at the unfolding tragi-comedy. How did I think I could turn back this tide of blood-lust?

What was I hoping for, a miracle?

Then, amid the blur and commotion, it happened.

They were shrinking from me.

They were calling the hounds away.

They were muttering about 'Bloody madman,' 'Loony-tunes,' 'Not all there.'

They were retreating.

It was a miracle.

An ABSOLUTE MIRACLE!

I chucked a few more stones for good measure, stopped flailing around, threw my head back and laughed like the lunatic they thought I was.

Back at the shed, I slumped on the floor beside you and heaved a sigh of relief.

"It's OK," I said, "They've gone."

You looked at me as if searching for reassurance.

"Really. They've gone. They won't be back for a while."

We locked eyes. I reached out my hand. You let me rest it gently on your head for a second. Then you were up, and trotting towards the open door. You stopped and looked back at me, and I thought I saw gratitude in those liquid gold eyes.

I sat on that shed floor for a long time, treasuring the memory.

All that drama happened only a couple of months ago. You stopped visiting for a while, and I tried not to worry that you'd been spooked. I still worked in the garden, but it wasn't the same.

A couple of weeks ago, I was doing some long-overdue weeding, when there was a familiar rustling in the long grass. I looked up and there you stood, as vibrant as the first time we'd met. What I wasn't banking on was the larger, reticent fox behind you. Seconds later, came pouncing, rolling, scampering, four little dark reddish-brownish balls of joyous fur. Cubs!

I felt a swell of pride. My girl did well!

Except you weren't my possession, and never would be. Your beauty was in your wildness. You sought me out. It was a privilege I'd never take for granted.

We locked eyes again, as we had all those weeks ago. This time I saw not just gratitude, but understanding.

We both knew that although I may have saved you once, you'd saved me every day I'd known you, Fire Fox.

GOLDFISH

BY SUSAN EMM

When Gerald reincarnated as a goldfish, he was somewhat surprised. It wasn't that he didn't have any appreciation for his new ability to swim underwater, or enjoy the occasional swish of his flexible fan tail. On the contrary, he was delighted with his sleek orange body. He also liked the solitude and space of his new home and had become accustomed to regular mealtimes and the taste and texture of flakes. An absence of worry about paying bills or keeping his wife happy were additional blessings. Perhaps it was churlish to complain.

What really upset Gerald was the absence of any logic or sign of proper reward. His new circumstances made no sense. Did his years of service as a bank manager, his membership of a prestigious golf club or charitable donations amount to nothing? A goldfish. It was so embarrassing. Then there were the storms to contend with. These could arrive without warning, tossing him about all over the place. Most unpleasant. His disappointment gradually gave way to acceptance. After all, who could he complain to?

There was something else bothering Gerald. An unsettling thing that sent shivers up his backbone. He could not escape the smudges of orange, brown and green that swirled before his eyes from the other side of the bowl. He tried to shake off a growing sense of discomfort that they looked familiar. Gerald's eyes grew larger. It was the wallpaper! That ghastly pattern. His wife had chosen it for their front room. Just to spite him. He was unable to escape the evidence of his own senses. Not only was he a goldfish. He was a goldfish swimming around in a bowl, plonked on a sideboard, looking out on his own front room.

One day, Gerald was taking a nap near the bottom of the bowl, when an unexpected vision of a spider floated across his unlidded eyes. He recalled the day a spider had appeared in the kitchen and made him drop the eggs he'd been unpacking. It had continued to reappear at the most inconvenient moments – like when he was having a shave or sitting on the toilet. He could still recall the discomfort he'd felt. At the time, he'd dismissed the ridiculous connection that his mind had made. Just because his mother-in-law had passed away the previous spring. His fish brain throbbed as he struggled to find new boundaries of possibility.

As time passed and was difficult to measure, Gerald concluded that he might discover a cure for cancer, solve world hunger problems and invent something to save the planet, but no-one would ever know. Then another thought occurred to him. Perhaps he would be able to take this knowledge with him into his next reincarnation! He began to fantasize. He'd be a genius. A champion. Rich. After all, he surmised, Einstein may have been a goldfish in a previous life too. Black holes? Fish bowls. Who knew? Gerald swam a victory lap.

Whoosh! Swoosh! Swish! Now what was it? Who am I? Hungry. Fly. Tasty. Ouch!

A goldfish was swimming in a bowl. A woman called Jennifer talked to the fish every day. She named it Gerald, in memory of her husband. Jennifer tapped the bowl. "Morning Gerald," she boomed. Receiving no reply, she moved closer and whispered,

"This wallpaper is giving me a headache. Do you mind if I change it?"

The silence made her sigh and wonder if perhaps it was time to get a dog. At least she would be able to take it for walks.

Jennifer stepped back and stood on a spider making its way across the carpet.

LASAGNE AND THE POT-BELLIED PIG

BY TRACEY JACOBS

The lasagne was in the oven, most of the kitchen cleared, now all Polly had to do was make herself look presentable. I say 'all'. Polly was one of these people who takes an absolute lifetime getting herself ready; removing make up, reapplying different shades of this and that, and changing the carefully-selected outfit time and time again.

At forty, being so picky and choosy, never settling for what is known as second-best, Polly had realised that she was alone. Which was alright at first because people muck you about, and she needed her space, her own things around her, everything in its proper place. If somebody asked her if they could stay the night, an inward panic attack occurred; they might move a cushion or an ornament.

Some would say Polly was obsessed. It very much sounds like it from what I've told you so far, doesn't it? Even as a child she had to know where her toys were, each book placed in a neat pile with the title visible, all the dolls' clothes neatly folded. I think that's cute and it's nice to know that she cared for her toys, as many children don't. Anyway, back to her getting ready.

Polly's hands were shaking as she attempted to apply black eyeliner, then mascara. This was the third attempt: first time it had made her look like a panda and second time even worse as it smudged, but still her trembling hands tried to grip the pencil steadily and it was becoming an ordeal. "Okay," she said aloud, "I'll try you again later." Some people do talk to their make-up you know. The lasagne smelt delicious but the clock was moving far too quickly. Then her mobile vibrated and made her jump so much the mascara stick went haywire and poked her in the eye. "No!" she cried. "This is doomed; this dinner date is definitely doomed." Oh, the dilemma! What does one do first? Clean up the face and eyes, or read a text? You guessed it:

'Hi Polly I am running l8 will explain l8r.'

That's just great then isn't it, she thought. *Oh well, I was getting in a pickle as always.* She ran downstairs to see to the oven, before dinner was a disaster as well.

Miraculously, the 'getting ready' went smoothly after that, apart from one or two changes of clothing. She was niggled that there was no kiss at the end of that text, come to think of it no name either! Good job she knew his name, and maybe the no kiss was because this was their first dinner together.

'Emmerdale' on, dinner under control, all she had to do now was wait.

Impossible. Polly could never wait patiently. Over the years she'd invented this way of making the waiting game go quicker. She looked around and made sure she knew where everything in the room was placed, great concentration needed, but it was always interrupted at about item number nine. Hopefully the placing game would take her mind off things now! But it did not. This man being held up for whatever reason was starting to gnaw at her. How rude! How can anyone be late for a first dinner date? Okay, these things happen, we all get held up for all sorts of reasons, but this was not fair. Dinner could be spoiled if he didn't get here soon. Then her mind worked overtime. *Oh, my God, he's married*, she thought, *that's it! He's having difficulty thinking of a reasonable excuse. Of course, that's the delay because his wife is questioning him! Yes, that's it, married – or with someone in a permanent way.*

Sadly, for Polly, most occasions went pear-shaped in some way. She panicked so much that any chance of a light-hearted get-together with friends, family or colleagues just became an ordeal! She had her therapy sessions, tried to remember all the advice, the tools as they called them, the stuff she should keep in her head to bring out when necessary. They made her head sound like a garden shed full of tools that you put away when not needed, which always made her smile. *Tools? Oh, at Christmas do we bring out the Hoe, Hoe, Hoe?* and that, you will be pleased to know, made Polly smile. You see? Just think of something comical and your mood can change.

Hoe, hoe, hoe, she thought and with that there was a knock on the door. She froze, *Oh my God it's him!* Well nobody else was due so it had to be the man.

She cleared her throat so it wouldn't sound like she'd been panicking. Fiddling with the key seemed to take an eternity, and of course her tiny hands were shaking and any onlookers would have been amused at the expression on her face! This was it, the moment was here, and there he was. After three weeks of online chat and guessing stuff about each other, there stood Alan. She thought he was so butt ugly the urge to shut the door was very strong, but he was stronger, and he shoved the door open and was in her hallway in no time.

"Evening Polly," he said, looking cheerful and confident. Before I go any further I must tell you that he had the most awful tight orange jeans on: his belly and the hairs on it were showing over the top. They had obviously been the reason he was late, as he would have taken hours to squeeze into them. *To be honest*, Polly thought *he looks like a pot- bellied pig*. Which is an insult to a wonderful creature!

"We meet at last, eh Polly? Sorry for the delay. I had a slight problem with me kid. He wouldn't stop hassling me 'cos I was wearing orange jeans, ha ha."

"And why are you then?" she asked tentatively. "I mean . . . w-w-wearing orange?"

"It's me lucky colour Doll, and by the look of you, it's workin'. Book the church or what? You're a babe darlin'. Summin' smells good."

All panic left her; they say it does in an emergency. Time for plan B: text her friend to come to her rescue. He was not at all like he described himself to be! But seriously, orange jeans that were too tight, passion killer or what!

If there was one thing Polly hated it was the word 'me' instead of 'my'. What on earth did he think he sounded like? Common as muck, that's what! Plus, he had never mentioned having a child in all their previous conversations.

Two hours later, all the lasagne had been scoffed. I say scoffed because a pig would have had more table manners. He burped, and slurped, and carried on talking about stuff that was ridiculous with his mouth full, of course. Polly was starting to panic. She'd sent numerous texts to her friend and left a couple of desperate-sounding voicemails. *Time to escape to the toilet again for yet another text.* Why hadn't Tessa turned up? She had promised profoundly that she would check her mobile regularly, and if needed would come straight away to help get rid of him. The last time they had had an agreement like this it had worked; that evening had gone well until the date, John, had decided to take his shoes off without asking, and plonk his stinky feet on the couch. Worst of all, he had a hole in his sock. *No way* Polly had thought, and sent a text immediately to get Tessa round. Between them, they made sure he left.

She did try to escape again, but at the eighth time it was becoming increasingly difficult.

"You got some sort of weak bladder or summin?" said Alan

"No, sorry. I do get a bit like this with new people, Alan. Kind of hyper," she said nervously.

"Well come and be hyper over here wiv' me then, Doll. Come to fink of it, maybe not so hyper when you take your clothes off, do that as slowly as you like. Got all night haven't we, Doll?" Then he did the most irritating laugh and sounded like a schoolboy embarrassed around his friends.

Polly decided that she would have to think of a reason to get him out, maybe something that they both could leave the house for and then, when she felt safe, tell him to do one! She was starting to lose her temper. The evening just hadn't gone to plan, and in her mind if he wasn't what she expected her plan B was to let her friend know and then be rescued. It was horribly unnerving that Tessa had not shown up. She couldn't take any more of his company *and* he kept doing smelly farts as well!

In the kitchen, she tidied around and kept busy. Every now and then he would shout out "'Ow much longer you gonna be, Doll?" This time, she was preparing dessert. At least that stopped him thinking about her slowly stripping.

Most of us would probably have run out, and gone to someone else we knew. I know I would have. Polly wouldn't dream of letting one of her neighbours see this gross fat man; the humiliation would have been too much to bear. It could only be Tessa.

Suddenly the fat pig was behind her, breathing down her neck, far too close for comfort, and she was chilled to the bone. *Get away from me* she said in her head.

"Do you like fresh cream?" she asked brightly, and with so much fake effort it sounded hilarious, and then she dropped the spoon, and cream went dripping down his leg.

"Woah! Careful Doll, watch what you're doin! These are me best jeans and now look at 'em," he shouted. His tone had changed from playful to angry in a flash.

"Oh, my God Alan, I am so sorry, I do get a bit clumsy when nervous, I did tell you that."

With that he started taking them off, no shame about how ridiculous he looked as he wriggled and twisted himself out of the tight orange things!

Then he went upstairs, slammed the bathroom door and locked it.

"Alan, I'm sorry. There's no need to be this upset. I can run them through the wash if you want. It will come out, please don't be angry with me." Polly hated that she had upset him and had to make it right. Earlier she had wanted rid of him, now she needed reassurance.

"Prefer to do me own washing fanks, your machine might be filthy."

"It is not!" she retorted smartly. "I clean it regularly and . . ."

"No, you ruddy well don't," he interrupted, "I saw limescale in the door bit and you ain't putting my best jeans in that shitty fing."

Polly was speechless. How *dare* anyone criticise the cleanliness of anything in her house; even though she must admit that she rarely cleans things like fridges, cookers or washing machines. How *dare* he say something like that, especially when she cooked such a lovely lasagne!

"You might be a good cook and lovely lookin', but that's it, I'd rarva watch paint dry than 'ave any more time wiv you. You ain't smiled once in the time I've bin 'ere." Alan sounded disappointed, almost close to tears. This situation had to be rectified.

"I am so sorry Alan, really I am. You see I get a bit highly strung sometimes, and I haven't met Mr Right yet, and I think I should have. Do you understand why I panic, Alan? I kind of tend to like my own space and it scares me. Is that so wrong?"

There was no noise coming from the bathroom. It was hauntingly silent.

"Alan, what are you doing? Please come out of there. This is silly, it's just a pair of trousers. I can buy you some more if that's what you want."

No response.

Forty-seven minutes later he opened the bathroom door.

Polly was sitting at the top of the stairs. He had put his beloved orange jeans back on. The stain hadn't been *that* bad, so why such a fuss? She wondered how on earth he'd managed to not make a sound while he squeezed himself back into them.

"Better be going now, Doll. Fanks for the dinner and half smile I think I got, unless I imagined that!" he said sarcastically.

"Oh, is that it then?" she asked in a surprised manner. "I thought we still had lots of talking to do."

"Nah. Not from me anyway, I carn't, Doll, as luvly as you are an all that. I just carn't."

"Why can't you, Alan? Why can't we try to understand each other?"

"I carn't talk to people like you, Doll, it, erm, it's just too hard...I 'ave a prob you see."

Polly didn't see. It seemed weird how she didn't like him at first, then a couple of hours later it was the opposite, just because she spilt cream down his jeans.

With that there was a knock at the door. She raced downstairs and couldn't be more pleased to see Tessa.

"At last! I texted ages ago. This has been a nightmare!"

"Polly, you sent me twenty-six texts and two voicemails. An improvement on last time, thirty-seven texts but just the one voicemail. This time you took eleven minutes longer to contact me. You're improving Polly. I think so anyway."

"What the hell are you on about, Tessa?" Polly didn't like the edge to Tessa's voice.

"The last escapade of you trying to find Mr. Right. You didn't even make it to twenty minutes before you heavily criticised the poor man."

With that Alan appeared and greeted Tessa like they were old friends. Polly looked confused.

"Yeah, we know each uvver. 'Ave done for years. You must've caught on at some point. Tess wouldn't let you 'ave any old stranger in again. 'Ow many we up to now Tess?" he laughed.

"Seventeen, Alan."

"What exactly are you two up to?" Polly looked from one to the other, confused.

"Showing you how ridiculous you are," Tessa said impatiently.

Alan nodded in agreement, "You need help Polly, you're a freak!"

With that Tessa took control, "Look Polly, this can't go on. Every week you ask me to come to your rescue, while you try to find Mr. Right. Trouble is you're looking for Mr Perfect. John was a lovely man, but you insisted he was smelly. There's always something stopping you. You're your own problem Polly, and you need help. I asked my cousin to chat to you online and we set this up. How did *you* like the criticism? Him telling *you* what he really thought, and overreacting to the slight accident? I planned it for you Polly. I had to, you're sick. I am *so* sorry." Tessa looked sorry as well, but went on to say that she'd had a gutful of her friend's behaviour.

"You always call me Tessa as well, and for years I have been saying 'Its Tess, drop the 'a', but no, it's always Polly's way."

Polly stood in the hallway staring in disbelief. *How dare they come into my home and treat me like this! They must hate me. They've been planning this for weeks. He was such a messy eater, he had orange stains on his chin! Urgh, most people would be careful about that, especially on a first date. What gives them the right to judge me so cruelly? Hypocrites!*

Polly's breath quickened, thousands of thoughts entered her head. Hands trembling, she picked up a dirty plate and went to hurl it at Tessa's head. Alan opened the door and ran out, leaving Tessa to face the confrontation. Suddenly she wasn't so brave and started to utter an apology. The plate never got thrown. For the first time in Polly's life those stupid 'tools' that she'd learnt came up trumps. This was amazing, a calm and collected Polly, and an anxious Tessa.

"Get out of my home and get a life of your own Tess," she hissed. "Oh and notice I dropped the 'a' at last. I think it's safe to say *you* need help. Not me. Goodbye Tess." With that Tess left hastily and quietly closed the door.

Polly looked at the mess in the kitchen, and was drawn to the washing machine. It looked clean enough. *Who the hell do these people think they are? And it hasn't been seventeen times! Although, wait a minute, yes it could be,* she thought, there were lots of names cropping up in her mind. *Justin, Sam, judgemental Rob . . . Bloody cowards, gutless wonders! After all the trouble I went to making such a delicious lasagne. At least I haven't got broken crockery too.*

"I will make sure they get their 'just desserts' though," she said through gritted teeth.

And we all know that revenge is a dish best served cold!

My Grandmother's Legacy

By Elizabeth Lee

My grandmother died. She quietly passed away at the age of ninety-eight, and left a fortune. An impressive town house and such a quantity of jewellery, fine furniture and other chattels as one might expect of such an important person. As her only grandson, my monetary portion was generous. She also left me her pet.

As children, my sisters and I had been fascinated by the little creature and would beg to play with it. Nothing had been seen like it before, and I have never heard mention of a similar beast, either in the real world, or in myth. It is a crossbreed; half-fox, half-hare. Formerly, she was more fox, but now the hare has become more dominant and she seems an equal blend of the two, quite different, beasts.

She is the size of a small dog, with a glossy coat of deep orange. Her belly and underparts are cream, and she has black tipped ears. Her tail is that of a fox, and she has a vixen's pretty, little face, although it is softer and rounder than is usual in reynard. Her long ears are leporine, as are her back legs. Her teeth are those of a canine, and she prefers to eat meat, although occasionally will graze on grass, looking cautiously around with her dark, lustrous eyes.

Her origins are a mystery. Family tradition tells us that my grandfather brought her back from one of his voyages to China, and gave her to his then-fiancée to keep her company while he was away. By whatever route she came into our family, it was many, many years ago, and she does not seem to age; the years wash over her without touching her in the slightest. She remains slender and clear of eye, and her fur retains its vividness, even on her muzzle.

She was devoted to the old man until his death, and mourned him for many years. She would sit gazing at his portrait and cry softly. She seemed to be fond of my grandmother, but only, I believe, because that redoubtable woman was adored by my grandfather. Family members were tolerated, but she was, and continues to be, extremely wary of strangers. She was always more willing to be close to me, and would sit happily on my knee for hours, much to the annoyance of my sisters, who longed to brush her silky coat and dress her up in their dolls' clothes. She was a strange distant creature; with us, but always apart in some way, unlike our family dogs, who rolled on the floor and played noisy games. She would never beg, or do tricks for us, and I never tried to make her. It would have been unthinkable to even attempt it. Her dignity defined her.

I found great comfort in this little animal and the bestowing of her affection on me. I was a quiet, bookish and withdrawn boy, unlike my gregarious, chattering sisters, and from the earliest age I knew I was destined to enter the family business. My life was mapped out before me, secure in our offices, and I would not be expected to embark on any dangerous sea voyages, unlike my predecessors. In fact, such escapades were strongly discouraged by this time, and I could look forward to a comfortable, settled life, marrying into another well-to-do family, and producing a brood of fine, respectable children. I was neither happy nor unhappy at this prospect; until, that is, I came of age and into my 'inheritance'.

On the day of my grandmother's death, my girl was delivered to our house in a basket, by a footman, with a letter from the old lady, wishing me well, and imploring me to care for her pet. I remember tipping him, and opening the basket, to see her crouching – uncertainty in her black eyes. She blinked up at me, and I smiled down at her. She stretched and put her dainty paws on the edge of the basket, asking to be picked up. I obliged and she snuggled up to me, her head on my chest. I could feel her heart beating and the steady rhythm of her breathing. I felt her sink into me and sigh with pleasure. Did I sense relief in her? A realisation that she was home? For sure, a wave of happiness washed over me and something inside me awoke, a longing to which I could not put a name.

During the next few months, which happened to be summer, I grew to know my companion and loved her more each day. She lived with me, side by side, and slept at night on my bed. I was no longer lonely – her soft sighs in the dark hours filled me with joy, and the way she woke me, with a gentle pat of her paw to the side of my face gave me a pleasure that I had never known before. She seldom, if ever, left my side. She dined with me, and would come visiting, and to church, sitting demurely on my knee, her pretty head tilted first to one side, then the other, listening intently to any talk. My parents objected occasionally to my little girl accompanying us, but I suppose they decided that as long as she did not interfere with my studies or my learning of the business, no harm was being done.

During the warm evenings, after my studies were done, and my office work completed, I would take my girl into the garden and lie on the grass, with her reclining beside me. We would sit for hours in the gently fading light, lazily watching the fish in the pond and enjoying the growing coolness of evening. She would come to sit on my lap and I would tell her of my studies, which were almost completed, and I would speak of work, of the comings and goings of our fleet, and she would nod with comprehension. I would share with her my modest hopes of happiness or perhaps, at this time, the hope that I would not be too unhappy trapped in this world.

I learned her little quirks and she began to communicate with me, to tell me something of her life, in her own way. She was totally alone in the world, she thought. An anomaly. She remembered nothing of her parents, or her early years, but often referred to her gratitude to my grandfather, who had, she considered, saved her from a life in freak shows or worse. She was afraid of foxes, and dogs in general, fearing their teeth and becoming their prey, but hares and rabbits shunned her, fearing her teeth and not understanding that she craved only their friendship. She was not too fond of cats, and other domestic animals bored her.

* * *

I spend a great deal of time caring for her. She loves to be groomed, and to be made as beautiful as I can make her. My sisters shake their heads and snigger behind their hands, but I don't care. Their opinion means less to me than ever before.

My little one obliges me by submitting to the leash, and we walk the streets, usually very early in the morning. She likes to visit the docks, and especially to see our ships. I take her on board, and during my conversations with the captain and crew, she will sit attentively, digesting all the information. When she has had enough, she stands up and stretches to get my attention. I make my excuses and we wander home through the wakening town, ready for our breakfast.

My love for her grows daily; I had been lonely. I did not fully understand until now but I had longed for a companion all my life. I am a person of specific tastes and find many of my contemporaries lack the seriousness and – how can I put it? – the *spirituality* that I desire in a friend. I know my duty is to marry, and of course, a loving wife and happy family should be my ultimate aim, but it isn't, not anymore. I understand now why she chose me, it is a partnership of mutual benefit. As I sit at my desk, watching her basking in a patch of sunlight, I think my heart will burst with love. Her orange coat glows like an ember and her sweet eyes gaze up at me with devotion.

I used to dread the cold damp of winter, but now it has become an utter delight to me. I go to my study after dinner, and I sit by a roaring fire, my girl on my knee. The family complain that they see less and less of me, but this is inevitable, and I'm preparing them for the day when I shall leave. They begin to weary me, with their incessant obsession with commerce and making money. They tie themselves tighter every day to the mundane and commonplace. I am loosening my jesses, and soon I shall fly.

I have been thinking; in fact, I do little else these days, but think. My darling has been telling me stories, whispering in my ear in her velvet voice, speaking of voyages and distant lands, of mountains, and deserts, vast expanses of wild moors, and deep forests. She tells me of strange people, of exotic animals, and of adventures. Of dark, hot nights spent sleeping under the stars, and of snow falling for six months of the year, of darkness at noon, and of sunlight at midnight. She speaks to me of all the things she has seen in her long, long life and it has made me yearn to see these wonders with my own eyes. And so I shall.

We are misfits, she and I. She taught me this and I shall be forever grateful. I understand that she will outlive me, and that pleases me greatly because I cannot imagine life without her. Lately, I barely communicate with my parents, and all my sisters do is look at me with pity, and shake their heads. They'll soon be married off, and will grow plump with their husbands, carrying on someone else's family line, breeding more respectable citizens for our merchant town. These latter days, people have begun to cross the road when they see me, and I know they talk behind their shuttered windows about what shame it is for my parents. I have heard whispers that my grandmother, in a final act of malice, cursed me with the bequeathing of her familiar, which is how the ignorant townsfolk view my darling girl.

Soon I will depart. Thanks to my grandmother's legacy, I have money enough and to spare; we will live well. No nagging wives for me, no whining children, no growing old and fat in a dull town, thinking only of my money and the face I present to the world. My darling has a desire to return to China, and I am strongly drawn to India. Maybe we will come back, maybe not. As long as I have my girl, I don't care. People say that I am mad, that I am bewitched, that I am a danger to myself, but my angel assures me, in her smooth, liquid voice, that I am not. I prefer to believe her.

Orange Chrysanthemum

By Claire Meakin

The slap of bare feet on sand permeated through the salty air, footprints left upon the beach like thousands of star-like grains. Each step filled her with increasing dread as she approached her certain fate. Dusky clouds swirled above her, spiralling and twisting in an ominous ballet. She outstretched a ghostly pale arm, feeling around in empty space. The place was familiar but her memory couldn't provide the answer. Regardless, the sea whispered for her to continue, as waves swept across the beach.

Her flame orange dress pirouetted in the coastal breeze, wrapping itself around her bare legs and slowing her down. It wasn't practical attire for a seaside walk; a dramatic, ornate amber robe, but the reason for her visit was hardly prosaic. She continued along the sands, hesitating and slowing occasionally.

She stopped. Her slender fingers felt something in the gnawing, stormy air. It was cold; far colder than the surrounding atmosphere. Smooth and brittle to the touch. She moved her hand so that the whole of her palm was pressed against it. Deep grooves were evident on the object's surface and she felt the sharp, precise edge of two equally sized hollows.

"What's there?" her soft voice called out, into the abyss of the beach.

A creaking and groaning echoed across the cliffs, like a machine whirring into life. The previously invisible item appeared slowly, as fragile bones came to life in front of her. It moved, shaking its head free of her hand.

"Is it time?" asked a deep, raspy voice.

She lowered her hand, her eyes wide and her breathing irregular and heavy. Its menacing smirk commanded her respect through pure terror; she was frozen to the spot.

"Time for what?" she replied.

Its face contorted into a smile to further emphasise a jaw full of yellowing, yet otherwise impeccable, teeth. Its eye sockets slowly closed shut, like eyelids, its delicate skull distorting to allow this facial expression. Then, after a pause, it laughed breathily in a way that could be mistaken for rapid tidal movements.

"I've been anticipating this moment."

Horror tiptoed down her spine causing her every muscle to jolt. Each nerve was alight, each hair was static and every inch of her skin was numb. There was no point in running, after all, she didn't know where she was, or why she was there. An inexplicable feeling told her not to resist, as though she no longer had control over herself. The skeleton lifted a bony arm, unfurled its fingers and placed its hand across her face. She clamped her eyes shut, an all-consuming blackness blanketing her.

"Relax, everyone has to do this."

Suddenly, she was falling, falling into the void. Opening her eyes, the previous darkness was replaced with oppressive flashing neon. The speed of her descent increased, causing the colours to blend into one blinding light. Then it stopped and her feet touched the hard ground.

She was standing on a station's platform, the noise of commuters filling her ears. She turned in a circle, trying to take in her surroundings. A young girl with brown pigtails was running alongside a train. She was screaming, tears cascading down her rounded, rosy cheeks.

"Mummy! Don't go! Wait!" Her pleas were no use.

A smart man with a briefcase knelt down next to the girl and attempted to calm her. It was no use, she was inconsolable.

The image collapsed around her, the child swirling into nothingness. It was replaced with a different scene. This time she was in a park, emerald leaves spiralling around her. The same girl, slightly older, wandered past, oblivious to her presence.

"Hey! Hey!" she screamed. "Listen to me! Stop!"

She knew what was going to happen, she had been here before. The girl was walking with a friend, talking and skipping through the flowers. Splash! The child's companion had fallen; fallen into a dirty pond. She couldn't swim. More screaming. More crying.

Once more, the vision disappeared and was replaced. A sitting room, parents, anger, arguing, fighting, blood, fainting, screaming, crying, black. A church, a coffin, a funeral, speeches, unfamiliar faces, screaming, crying, black. School, shouting, insults, pushing, stealing, hunger, screaming, crying, black. The process repeated and repeated until she was in the few moments she could remember before she arrived on the beach.

She was in the passenger seat of a taxi, seated next to herself. Past-her had a phone in her hand, her gaze focused on a rain soaked window and her seatbelt dangling, unattached, by her side. Outside of the window, cyclists and cars swerved to avoid the path of the speeding taxi while the road blurred into a whooshing grey mass; she was in a rush and had no reluctance in telling the driver this. She texted her father, telling him she would be late. Her awful time-keeping was infamous amongst her friends and family; it wasn't something she was proud of. Present-her's eyes widened. This is what had happened.

The taxi took a corner at great speed, too great a speed. The driver slammed his foot onto the brake but the taxi refused to stop.

The black bonnet of the vehicle crashed into brickwork, exposing wires and pipes. The wires snapped, sending branches of electricity into the frame of the vehicle. The prongs of current skipped along the surface, like a miniature thunderstorm. Then, it hurtled into the gas pipe which hissed in protest and mixed with the petrol. Bang! Fire licked up the paintwork, melting the metal, biting at the fabric seats. Past-her screamed. This was it. After everything, this was it.

The heat from the flames was unbearable as it gnawed on the flesh of her hands. She shook her arm but it was no use, the scent of burning meat filled the space. It was over so quickly but the memories were so vivid. Within the span of less than a minute, the only thing she knew, the only thing she was certain of, was ripped forcibly from her.

Present-her was the one screaming now, screaming like she had done in the past. All of her nightmares, all of her worst times had been shown to her like a macabre film where the plot was the most depressing things the director could think of. Blackness engulfed her for the last time, and instead of sinking she was flying. Rising higher and higher, watching the myriad of tears plummet into the endless night.

She gasped and stumbled backwards. She had returned to the beach, where *it* was waiting politely, hands tucked behind its spine.

"Why? Why did you do that?" she wailed sinking to the sand.

"Don't cry."

From anyone else, the statement could have been reassuring. Its tone of voice never altered, it was utterly emotionless. It offered her a decayed hand, which she accepted and used to stand up. It let go once she was up, but something was still in her grasp. She opened her palm to see the squashed petals of a flower. The image of hordes of all-black clothing and a wooden coffin with a sea of orange at its foot floated into her consciousness.

Orange chrysanthemums. Her mother's favourite.

Her feet ached suddenly and she jerked her eyes down. There was no skin, nor muscle, nor nerves on them, only off-white bones remained. She wanted to scream but those last minutes had taught her that no matter how much of that she did, the outcome would still be the same. The feeling was soon gone in her legs, torso, arms, hands, neck and finally her face. Her long, velvety chestnut hair tore out of her scalp and plunged to the ground. Her dress slipped from her shoulders and tumbled around her ankles.

"You can come with me now." The other one linked its arm in hers.

The two skeletons, hand in hand, strolled along the sands.

PETER

BY ANNA SPAIN

Orissa writes in her bedroom.

I live in a town near Orange next to the Blue Mountains,
William of Orange is part of my lineage,
Google says there are 20 places in the world called Orange; there isn't
one in England,
My room at 23 Chadwick Road, London E11 will be the 21st place.

"Greg, Rachael, let's celebrate the orange and have an orange week. Please say yes." Orissa's voice resonates down the stairs and into the hall of the seen-better-days high-ceilinged Victorian semi.

Gregory, youthful, wiry and freckled runs up the stairs. "What? Why do you want an orange week?"

Rachel's heavy footsteps leave her room. "What's going on now? I was cleaning out Peter; his tank has gone quite green."

Orissa, teases, "They say an orange a day keeps the doctor away."

"Really Ori! It's an apple a day, as you know."

"Maybe an orange is more likely to have a touch of the elixir. My Great Aunt Antoinette had freshly squeezed orange every day and she lived to 103. Did I tell you that we buried her wearing grass skirts and flowers round our necks, sashaying to tropical melodies?"

Rachael and Gregory in stereo, "Yes Ori. You did."

Melanie joins the group on the landing. "Orissa if you seriously want to go ahead with this idea let me know your plan."

Downstairs Leonora talks to Ricky. "Did you get that? Orissa is going to have an orange week. It sounds mad and fun. I'm gonna join in," says Leonora, "what about you?"

"Maybe. It depends if it's all about Orissa. You lot swarm around her as if she's the queen bee. Remember she is in here for a reason and it ain't good."

"Yeah right, Ricky, and you're the prince of lightness and kindness, are you?"

"Piss off," says Ricky, then storms into the kitchen.

Buy orange paint, dye and food.
A wicked, cruel queen wants to stop my orange week and a vain troll with orange hair is angry - he hates blending into the wallpaper.
Troll. O troll, hidden against the wall
Orange hair like a gangster's moll
Little short legs, not very tall
Last years pet is this year's troll.

A file stored in the office is Orissa's early personal history:

Born in Jamaica. Abandoned in the Blue Mountains by her Uncle Aidee.

Mother alerts the police to her five-year old missing daughter.

Found two days later tied to a tree; she does not talk and is silent apart from the occasional humming.

Moved to London, England, in 1995, age seven, to live with her Grandmother where she can receive specialist trauma support for children.

Orissa retreats to her bedroom and ritually reaches under her bed for the tired brown leather case, slowly opens the lid and picks up the photograph of her Ma and Pa. The photograph has faded over the years and the edges are tatty and worn by her yearning caress. Her ribcage stretches and lifts to the sound of a deep sigh.

Orissa walks into the office.

"Hi Melanie, here is my list of orange food."

Marmalade
Baked beans
Sweet potatoes
Red Leicester and Shropshire Blue
Carrots
Doritos
Tomato soup
Orange lentils (orange lentils with orange coloured mash)
Tinned Spaghetti
Apricots
Food colouring to make bread / cakes / mash
Cornflakes

"Wouldn't it be funny if my poo turned orange? Maybe I could do a poo sample each day; I will call it the Orange Poo-ohm-meter." Laughter ensues, excited from Orissa, uneasy from Melanie.

Later that day Orissa and Rachael shop for orange items. They talk while walking down the leafy suburban street to the High Street on a late summer day, warm with a light breeze.

Orissa confides in Rachael. "You and Greg have become my good friends. I'm still unsure of Leonora and to be honest I'm a bit scared of Ricky. I have this horrible feeling about him."

"Ori, he wouldn't be in the house if he wasn't ready for community rehab. Did you know that I'm preparing to move out soon?"

"Rachael! No, you can't leave us." Orissa tucks her arm through Rachael's and pulls it tight to her.

"Hey! Let's pick a name for the orange week. O'ruge, or Oralina – how about Oolala?"

"Yes. Oolala is great, it has a French ring."

They walk arm-in-arm saying out loud in a French accent "Oo-la-la, Oo-la-la . . ." laughing and smiling, enjoying a brief respite before the murky brown soil of the mind where slugs grow and fatten contentedly overtakes the flash of summer fun.

Dress in orange clothes (Rachael will make me a jump suit – bought fur fabric)
Eat orange food (bought dry goods)

Live in an orange house (paint my room orange – tomorrow and Thursday)

Have an orange pet (I can borrow Peter the goldfish)

Make new orange friends (bought orange card – make over the next week)

That evening Orissa begins drawing the orange people. One week on there are five families of cut out orange people in her suitcase.

The Orange Week

Day 1.

Orissa quickly lifts the lid of the brown leather suitcase.

"Good morning Mr and Mrs Orange Bird. How are Lincoln, Leticia and Lionel?" The cut-out family nestle inside a large scrapbook. "Ah, there you are Leticia. What's that stain round your mouth; did you eat chocolate after you brushed your teeth? Grandma would say to me, 'use soap and water and give it a good hard rub', and then she'd kiss the tip of my nose."

Leticia lies in her palm while she tries to gently rub the brown mark away with cotton wool and water. The card rips and the head is gone! Orissa is stilled, inanimate; her body shudders then she begins to sob. Sobs that grip and violently shake her, ribs heaving, back arched. Her mouth gapes, open silent as a goldfish, grief as hard as a glass bowl slides in with no space for sound. Leticia is lifeless in her outstretched palm; the round naive orange line-drawn head on the carpet staring upwards.

Hands on the clock continue moving, her world stops momentarily as grief and terror climb up the spiral staircase of her mind. Years of counselling rescue her as she moves back into consciousness; brushing tears away she reaches for her makeup bag and grasps the red lipstick that oozes the plastic sunshine smile. The red slides across, transforming blubber to pretty flower. She glances at the ticking clock and knows her deception does not fool the evil queen that barks from within.

Orissa stands outside Rachel's door, hands clenched to stop them shaking, knuckle poised, then falters. Second time is a success. Knock-knock on the bedroom door.

"Rachel, could I borrow a needle and some orange thread please?" says Orissa

Rachel calls out, "Come in Ori. Yes, help yourself, there's my sewing basket."

Back in her room she manipulates the needle, sharp-tip piercing the paper; prick-pull-stop, her eyes barely blinking as she stares at the cotton as it moves through the neck. Prick-pull-stop. Adroitly she sews until the head is reattached, humming as she works.

"Leticia, you can eat all the chocolate you like; we've both got scars now. Look at my arms." Her hand trembles as un-safe jelly as she carefully pushes up her shirtsleeve to reveal the hidden thick wealds of self-destruction.

Day 2.

Orissa lies in bed looking at the ticking clock. Whispering, so that no one can hear, "I have new friends that you can't harm evil queen," tick-tock, tick-tock, tick-tock. "They're safe in my father's suitcase where your powers cannot reach. You can tick-tock off."

She unlocks the suitcase. "Good morning Louis Little-Satsuma, did you dream last night? I did."

"I walked down to the River Thames and as I crossed Tower Bridge a boat went underneath while the sails floated like gossamer over the top of the bridge, just a few feet in front of me. An orange monkey was on top of the mast and in his hand was a book of Tangerine Dreams. As he opened the book a large fish leapt out of the page – it looked at me with a wide, ugly, menacing grin then leapt off into the river. The sails and boat became one as it left the bridge and carried on down the river. Words from the pages floated off into the water, 'poor thing, poor thing,' whirlpools pulled the words down,

.   poor
                                          thing

          dear girl

                                  poor
                                          thing

Louis, Louis Little-Satsuma, I may need your help as I feel those fish are nasty and evil. Could Peter of Orange be part of a plot, what do you think?"

Lithe body and feet run down the stairs; physicality strong, mind-weakening, struggling to reach out of the descending spiral.

"Morning everyone," says Orissa. "I'm cooking this evening for our house dinner."

"I'm looking forward to an orange dinner," says Rachael.

"It will be a first for me," says Greg, "yum-yum!"

Crockery chinks and clinks. CRASH. The bowl slips from Ricky's clasped hand. Orissa glances at the broken crockery on the floor and dashes an anxious glance towards Rachael – then screams.

"Ricky, put the knife down. It's not funny," says Leonora.

He grins, as he holds a knife to the orange. "Look at that stupid face drawn on the orange. It needs a knife in it – it's fake. You're all fake trying to pretend that you're normal. An orange week is the most stupid thing in the world and I don't want any part of it."

Melanie rushes into the room. "What's going on in here?"

"Its Ricky. He's being stupid. He's jealous of Orissa," says Leonora.

Ricky is absent from the dinner party.

Day 3
Orange is seeping into my toenails, toes and feet, crawling up my legs and thighs. Then waits.

Orange that thrums with vitality

Trees hanging with orange baubles of sweet-segmented juice, trapped in transparent membranes

Juice trapped, orange trapped on the tree

Tree trapped in the forest

Rescue the tree

Day 4.
Orissa reaches into her under-bed suitcase of dreams.
"Good morning Mrs Honey Peach-Bottom."

Day 5.
Orange is seeping into my fingernails, fingers, hands and arms. It caresses my armpits seeking a place to hide. The orange knows of the lymph nodes for good or bad, it is undecided and waiting for the final call.

Day 6.

I need to talk to Peter.

Orissa speaks rapidly, "Hello, Rachael, hello. Can I borrow Peter please, as I would like to draw some orange fishes for the party tomorrow? Can I please?"

"Yes, he's in the tank; go into my room," says Rachael. "Shall I make us some tea and we can do some drawing together and make bunting for the house party?"

"All right."

"Be back in five mins," says Rachael.

Orissa closes the door.

"Peter, Peter of Orange, I have five minutes to talk to you. Please tell me about the big, evil, grinning fish in my dream. I dreamt of it again last night. Shall I hold you so that you can whisper in my ear? Come here, Peter." Her hand thrusts into the tank, fingers grasping like an octopus, grabbing Peter, and lifting him out of the water.

Heavy footsteps walk up the stairs.

"Ori, what are you doing? Put him back in the tank, now," Rachael bellows.

"I was only talking to him."

"And was he talking back to you?"

"He was about to, but you spoilt it by coming in."

"Peter is a fish, he can't talk to you; he's just a fish."

Orissa runs out of the room and slams the door behind her.

The house hushes as whispered talk settles in corners, eyes and ears chasing the changes. Alert, amber, watchful.

Day 7

Party day.

At seven p.m. neighbours and friends begin arriving, bringing orange edible gifts. Music plays and an upbeat mood of chatter and laughter ripples through the house. The orange and mango punch hits the spot.

Greg gathers the guests into the kitchen for the hot savoury dishes. Pumpkin quiche and kedgeree. Smiling faces watch the feast of orange food.

Ricky had prepared a special dish. A-dish-to-be-served-cold.

Orissa comes down the stairs, head to toe in orange fur fabric – in her hand lies Peter the goldfish with a skewer run through his middle. Blood pools into her hands, the orange sleeves turning emergency red.

Can a goldfish have this much blood?

Silence.

Rachel rushes up and slaps her around the face, "How could you kill him?"

Orissa begins to hum so loudly that the music is drowned out.

Ricky stands in the doorway, a malevolent grin on his face.

As sly as the fox, self-satisfied and smug.

POLLY AND THE GUARDIANS

BY VALERIE TYLER

Polly clung to an upturned boat. Coldness of wet brown wood pierced her fingers. Having no sense of time or direction she'd drifted away from the planned route. Blackness of night engulfed her like a cold, heavy blanket. Water lapped against her legs, the pain more bearable as they became numb. She felt alone, empty, far away from civilisation. After sliding down the boat she managed to haul herself further up again. Her twenty-year-old body felt heavy as a wet rag and weak with exhaustion.

What a fool I've been to contemplate this journey alone, thoughts screamed into oblivion. She called to the stars, Universe, God and the guardians of the galaxy. "Where are you now?" Her eyes flickered before closing.

Water tapped her shoulder awakening her. She pulled herself up in time to see clouds roll across the moon. A dark magician of night pulled back his burly cloak allowing beams of light to fall on her hands. Glancing at their bone structure, hardly recognisable, her eyes followed the pathway of veins to the ends of white fingertips.

Polly noticed a small triangular shape. Remembering now that she'd caught her tee shirt on a nail. *Had this saved me?* Her body had sprawled across soaking wood, her tee shirt clinging to this nail but as she had slid further down it had eventually pulled away leaving the tiny fragment still clinging. She focussed on the small piece of orange cloth, its brightness provoking memories.

Her consciousness wandered in and out of dreams, seeing the orange dress she'd worn to school on the one day her uniform wasn't ready. Miss Trampton stood there with hands on hips, wearing a three-cornered hat and vivid red lipstick which reminded Polly of the Queen of Hearts from Lewis Carrol's 'Alice in Wonderland.' It was a dream.

Miss Trampton had no heart. She was tall, thin, very plain and pasty looking, she didn't wear lipstick but always had her hands on her hips, plaits pinned on top of her head. Polly wondered if she ever let her hair down, and washed it or brushed it. That wasn't a dream.

"How dare you come to school dressed in those colours Miss Polly Fletcher? Detention for you!" The whole class had turned their heads and giggled behind their hands.

"But Miss . . ."

"No buts and no excuses. If we all made up reasons to dress down what would become of the world?" She wasn't interested in reasons.

Polly visualised a world with no school uniform, with no rules, but best of all, with no Miss Tramptons. Gazing into space earned detentions. She'd thought of her mother lying in the hospital bed, and her aunt Kate chucking clothes to her that morning, telling her it was best she went to school, there was nothing she could do to help. That wasn't a dream either.

Gazing again during detention was interrupted by Trampton's voice.

"There ain't nuffin' out there gonna help you. That's pure space up there, nuffin' else at all, even scientists'll tell you, so I suggest you just get on wiv what I've told you to do. You are and, if you don't buck your ideas up, always will be, an under-achiever."

Then she strutted like a colourless peacock from the room.

Polly believed in universal truths, that we're all part of a living, breathing cosmos. She wondered if she was the only person alive that knew the identity of the Guardians. She heard them sometimes, the weird but wonderful noises echoed through her mind telling her of the ancient knowledge they carried. *If only others believed in them,* she thought. She thought a lot, her mind often focussed on a different plane. They communicated with her, helping overcome traumas in life. Her mother had taught her to call on them when life felt cruel or when she felt unable to cope. "They'll always come, just believe."

Visualising blue eyes gazing from under the hat's brim with the same love they'd always had, she recalled the comfort of her mother's voice. "Whatever makes you happy and peaceful in life, no matter whether big or small, it's the greatest achievement you'll ever make. Never be afraid to ask. Don't do everything alone, or doubt your worth, and never be scared to call on the Guardians of the Galaxy. They truly exist in many forms, different for each of us."

She wished her mother was there now. Polly's world was dark, forbidding and untrusting. She embarked on adventures alone, afraid of not reaching others' expectations.

Her thoughts drifted back, wondering how strange it was that Miss Trampton's voice changed to a cockney accent when there was no one else about. If it expressed a pet hate for those that didn't reciprocate her demands, Polly was one of them. Underachieving in some subjects, she excelled in sports and gymnastics, being gifted with great stamina, but she'd never been offered the right opportunities to excel as the schools she attended didn't prioritise anything other than the three R's. Pressurised teachers aimed for outstanding results, but not in gymnastics and sports.

During detention Polly sang, 'I believe in Angels', then defiantly changed the words and replaced Angels with orange, feeling annoyed that her favourite dress had become the target of an insult. She was made to write a hundred lines of 'I must not wear orange to school.' The last line read, 'I believe in orange.' On leaving the building, she doubted if anyone would even look at them. The next day she visited her mother in hospital, had the rest of the week off with stomach pains, and was glad for the last week of term. She wouldn't encounter Miss Trampton again, though the effects of her harshness were ingrained forever. Confidence knocked, but determination took front place.

Polly's awareness returned. Focussing on the orange triangle again, she realised she was still trying to prove something to the Miss Tramptons of the world by risking this journey to Fog Island alone. Its name was due to the heavy mist that surrounded it; a mystical place, but also sometimes dangerous to visit. The main visitors were nearby fishermen who took advantage of the abundance of sea-life and the familiarity of the area. The small boat had been salvaged from scrap. She trusted it to finish this journey that was in dedication of overcoming let-downs. It would prove that she could achieve, and that people's aims can be different, but still worthy. This was also dedicated practise as part of her essential training, before joining others in a charity rowing expedition only two weeks ahead.

Had the queen of hearts been right after all, and trying to prove my worth could have a fatal end?

A strange but familiar noise loomed from under the boat. Water near her became turbulent, as if disturbed by something large; *maybe there's a shark, is this my end?* She attempted one last guardian call. "Please help me!" She listened for signs. Preparing for goodbye she glanced upwards, her mind sang to the stars before she slumped completely unconscious. Only she heard the song.

In the distance three fishermen watched a school of dolphins leaping and sounding their call. A clearing grew in the mist. "Now isn't this the most amusing sight you've ever seen?" said one.

Then another "It's unusual to find 'em so close to the beach." They glanced around.

"There's no sign of anything at all in the water around 'em. It could be dangerous for 'em to be so close to shore. I wonder what brings 'em in this far, 'tis a mystery." They started to move close to the creatures who enticed them almost to the water's edge.

Then as quick as an eye can blink the dolphins frantically danced, leaped and nose-dived back out to sea.

The three men looked on in relief realising the dolphins were safe. "I wonder what that was about?" said one, tipping his hat from his forehead and wiping sweat from his brow. "Seems they were tryin' to tell us somethin'."

As they pulled the boat to shore they noticed something on the beach. Rushing over to take a look they saw dishevelled clothing. Wet, torn black hair mingled with seaweed. It was difficult at first to make out what it was.

"My God, it's a woman!" The tallest of three bent down to take her pulse. "She's still breathin','n what's this in 'er 'and? 'Ow did she get 'ere 'n 'all? There be no sign of a boat or anythin.' Quick, pass me the water."

Polly felt the gentle touch of a hand, something she hadn't felt for a long time.

Her fingers slowly uncurled, revealing a tiny orange square. Her mouth trembled, "Am I dead, is this Heaven?"

"No lass, its Fog island you be landed on, 'n as strange as it sounds, it seems you were 'elped by dolphins. If it wasn't for them we wouldn't 'av found you."

"The Guardians of the Galaxy! How incredible they are," she spoke quietly.

"What's she sayin?"

"Don't you know? The dolphins are the Guardians of the Galaxy," she replied. "Well for me, anyway." A smile appeared on Polly's face, making her look beautiful. Much to their surprise she began to sing. In her mind, she had defeated all the Miss Tramptons of the world. A sudden realisation came to her. *There are people in this world that care, there are ones that I can trust.*

None of them saw the woman standing nearby on the rocks watching them from under the brim of her hat and smiling back.

Popsicle Days

By Karen Leopold Reich

Petticoat torn and wheeled away,
Revealing stout, flame-washed flesh
On sticks
We licked,
Tongues a-fire,
Lips numbed
Mouth hugging
Ice incandescence
Sensing
Browful drumcrash
In the fever-dash
To swallow summer's promise whole
Silk smoking breath at heat's embrace
No rein on passion or escape
From time's toll
As the sheen of sweat
Wet-marked the cresting of delight
The soft slush dribble
Last auburn flare
Last orange fluorescence,
Reverescence,
In the wild rust stain
Sickle-framing a smile.

PREDICTIVE TEXT.

BY VALERIE TYLER

If I desired you, your colour would be orange, however I do not. Silly predictive text, please leave me alone. Wherever I go you seem to follow. Are you determined for me to wear a crown of stupidity? I thought I was the queen of spellings. Maybe your aim is to lure me into being the bride of stupid mistakes. I find it quite strange how insistent you are on getting things right, yet you are nearly always wrong; except for a few times maybe, such as when you turned 'perhaps' into 'poo' and 'lets' into 'liar'. How did you know what I was thinking? You even turned yourself into 'productive', trying hard to fool me. I asked you to disappear and you turned it into 'disappointed'. Though I've said before now that there's no such word as 'can't', could it be possible that you heard me? Because you substituted 'can't' with 'cantaloupe'. I found myself looking the word up, and now I know that Cantaloupe refers to a variety of the Cucumis melon species. It originally referred to non-netted, orange-fleshed melons of Europe. They are an excellent source of vitamin C and A in the form of carotenoids. They also contain B vitamins, folate, vitamin K, magnesium and fibre. Oh, and potassium, but don't take my word for it, google it as I have just done. I read that orange fruits can prevent cell damage and aging. Can you see how distracted I've become?

(Anyone who is reading this, I do not claim to be a nutritionist and know nothing of these things, but if you care to look the information up for yourself, or visit a qualified nutritionist, that would really appease old predictive.)

You put yourself in most obscure places, bringing nothing but nonsensical meaning to all who observe you with intelligent eye. You bring chaos and arguments with your insults. Sometimes – most times – you lie about what people are saying, jumping in quickly, taking advantage of those in a hurry, too busy to notice you have changed the dialogue completely.

Giving reason for some to say, "How underrated learning has become and how ignorant people are these days! They have no knowledge of the real English language."

I imagine you to be laid in your bed of sentences, laughing at the frustration you've caused. I, for one, would gladly delete you if I knew how to. Predictive text, you slow me down with your unwanted intrusion, holding writing at an unbearable pace; comparable to being stuck in a traffic jam.

You are not orange and you are not a cantaloupe. Why do you even exist?

PUMPKIN FACE

BY KAREN INCE

"And that's why it has to finish here." The finality in Darius' voice matched his steady gaze. Sudden darkness. A heartbeat of silence, then applause. Bright lights flooded back. We filed on stage as rehearsed, bowed; bowed again. The beat of my heart echoed applause in my ears. I had played my part – admittedly a small part – in creating a different world for our audience to enjoy. I wanted to shout, sing, dance. I wanted to hang on to that moment; preserve it somehow to make it last forever. The applause died down, and I dutifully followed everyone else backstage to noise and chaos; hugs and congratulations. Such contrasts within a few feet: the all-over glare of fluorescent tubes instead of focussed stage lighting; cool air from the open windows a welcome relief after the heat of the spotlights; excited voices talking over each other in place of the orchestrated audience reactions and applause; the precision-rehearsed moves of onstage performance now lost among too many bodies in too small a space, all trying to get changed and collect scattered belongings.

The last three nights had been similar, but tonight, the final night, was even more intense. Some people were already talking about their next project; others still reminiscing about the last one. I couldn't join in. This had been my stage debut, I had nothing to compare it to. The adrenaline surges hadn't left us; the fever of excitement was still tingling in the air. I finally understood why people were so passionate about performing, willingly putting in so many hours of hard work.

"Listen up." The director's voice broke my fragile hold on my precious bubble of excitement and achievement. "As soon as you're changed, we need to strike and clear. The more hands helping, the quicker we can all get to the pub."

I understood approximately half of what she said, which mirrored my experience of the last few months. Whenever I thought I had mastered the theatre lingo, someone would catch me off guard, but I was sure that 'strike and clear' was new because it sounded more like some kind of ninja assassin move than anything theatrical. I didn't ask. I didn't want to look more stupid than necessary. The bit about the pub was straightforward and I was motivated for whatever this strange ritual was we had to complete before we could go.

Back in my everyday clothes, I folded my cumbersome costume for the last time, draped it over my arm and headed back on stage. How quickly the space had changed; now lit like a normal room, the tiered seating empty, the magic of theatre dispelled. Everyone was busy sorting all the costume, props and furniture into piles with different destinations. Was I really the only one who had no idea how to help? Petra spotted me, and that all changed. "Cathy, love, put your costume over there – right, the pile to go back to the hire company. No, not that pile that's – yes, that one. Good. Now, what else? Oh, the head. Could you?"

Could I what? Petra tended to assume people would finish her sentences for her. I knew what head she was talking about. Somehow, it had become my responsibility.

Let me backtrack. The production required a head. A beheaded head. Though that doesn't really make sense. The head that had previously belonged to a beheaded body I suppose. But I digress. There were many challenges to be met that I couldn't help with, but at one famous – to me anyway – rehearsal I had a brainwave.

One of the many things I had needed to learn about the world of theatre, amateur or otherwise, was just what went into a production. In the past, I had enjoyed watching other people perform this mysterious craft from my comfortable seat in the audience. I'd never given any thought to costumes, furniture and so on. Well, except a couple of times when they seemed blatantly wrong. I discovered that any object which is used by an actor is called a prop, and that scenery is a specific term that doesn't include the furniture you see on stage. I learned that actors wish each other good luck by saying 'Break A Leg' and won't say the name of 'The Scottish Play', although it's perfectly all right to talk about the character Macbeth. And that before every rehearsal they do a warm-up for body and voice. Some of the exercises are quite similar to what I've done at the gym. And some are weird and definitely only belong in the theatre. My favourite, mainly because it made me laugh every single time, was a warm-up for the facial muscles called Pumpkin Face – Peanut Face. Pumpkin face is wide; open eyes, open mouth as big and round as you can possibly be. Peanut face is the opposite. Scrunched up and wrinkly and tiny. The director calls out one, then the other, then back and forth. It's fun. Try it.

And it was obvious; my one brilliant contribution to the production outside of my somewhat dubious acting ability. I'd spoken up. Pumpkin face – or rather pumpkin head. We could use a pumpkin as the basis of the bodiless head, with the addition of a wig. It had the right size and weight. Well, the right size. I don't know how heavy a head is.

And there it was. I had the job. I called myself the "Head of Head Procurement". It has a ring to it.

Buying a pumpkin is easy. I added it to my weekly shopping list. The kids thought it was Hallowe'en again, and were so disappointed when I told them it wasn't that I ended up buying them 'treats' anyway. There were plenty of old wigs in the wardrobe department. I chose a long black one that was the nearest match to Emily, my friend who played the girl who had to be beheaded.

The plan was to wrap it in a carrier bag full of blood. Stage blood. No-one expected me to donate. At the appropriate moment, it would be produced on stage looking like – well, a bloody head in a bag. I got creative with my make-up. I wanted it to look more like Emily, who's the reason I'm involved in this madness. Even though it would only be seen as a shape inside a bag, I took some strange comfort from knowing the pumpkin's make up was flawless. Rehearsals went well. The pumpkin was a hit. The grisly scene played out as expected. Dress rehearsal is the final one; the big one before the first public performance. We added the blood for the first time. All well and good. At the end of rehearsal, we put everything in place ready for the next night. And Darius dropped the bag with the pumpkin. Most of the blood stayed in it, which was lucky, and we were able to top it up the next night. But in amongst the blood, we didn't realise the lovely hard pumpkin shell was cracked.

Opening night came and went in a blur. I debuted. I remembered my words – well most of them. The audience at large were delighted; friends and family pleasantly surprised at my competence. We reset everything for the second night and went home. Second night, same again; feeling more confident now, I even got my words in the right order. Third night and I was feeling seasoned; I could get myself on and off stage at the right times without reminders. The final night and I nailed it. Entrances and exits, lines, moves, the works. I wanted to celebrate. But now I had to deal with that bloody head.

I found the bag. Something didn't look right. I opened it. And recoiled. The heat of the theatre lighting and the moisture of the stage blood trapped inside the plastic bag meant the inside of the pumpkin was now mush. Bad smelling mush. I looked for Petra. I wanted to ask her what I should do; how I should dispose of it. I couldn't see her. Everyone else seemed intent on their own tasks. I hesitated. The bag smelt. I needed air. I left the theatre, walking purposefully towards the nearest public bin. Out here, the smell was fainter.

I hesitated. Truly, I did think twice about whether this was wise. I glanced around. No-one was watching. I shoved the bag in the bin and walked hurriedly away. I felt like I really was trying to dispose of a gory head.

I met the others in the pub. We celebrated. We – that is I – drank too much gin. I took a cab home. Responsible me. I slept off the adrenaline, the excitement, the gin.

In the morning, I realised that in my hurried departure the night before, I had left a bag in the dressing room, containing my makeup among other things. I have other makeup; maybe too much. What can I say? It's a weakness. I really wanted what was in that bag. After downing a strong black coffee or two, I headed to the theatre. My theatre. I had trodden the boards and felt a sense of belonging, though I was a bit hazy whether the theatre belonged to me or I to it.

There was quite a crowd milling as close as they could to the cordon. What was happening? Like Chinese Whispers, the rumours started spreading. There's been a murder. What? In my theatre? No! Next rumour; the body's been chopped into pieces. How gruesome! In this lovely quiet market town? They've found the head. The head? Yes. In the bin. Outside the theatre. Very dramatic –there's always one person ready with a quip. Not much left of it. Blood and hair mainly. I left as unobtrusively as I could. I don't think Am Dram's for me, after all.

RANSOM

BY KIM HAMMOND

Fiona woke. She went to clasp her hands around her thumping head to ease the throbbing and realised she couldn't move. She heard the rattle of chains and something pinched her skin. "What the . . ?"

She opened her eyes but could see only a blackness. Was it dark? Night time? No, there was something strapped across her eyes. She kept falling in and out of consciousness and had no idea how long she was awake or asleep for.

Where am I? What's happening?

She was lying on something cold and damp, firm and lumpy. Her body was curled into the foetal position, her hands tied in front of her, her legs tucked tightly against her abdomen, feet tied together.

She could hear someone breathing and sensed she was not alone. A whisper? A woman's voice? Against the sound of dripping water she could just make out in the background, Fiona strained to hear. She didn't recognise the voice but could just make out the woman's words. "Are you sure Hardy will pay?"

Hardy. My father. The gangster.

Daddy Darling. Who never took much notice of her. Daddy Darling. Who would rather be out scheming and making deals than at home with her. Daddy Darling. Who probably wouldn't even realise she was missing.

Why would he realise? He liked to make out he kept a close rein on her, but he didn't care what she was up to and where she was. His henchmen meant more to him than she did. He insisted on knowing where they were every second of the day. But his only daughter – he couldn't give a damn.

His family. His gangster family.

They were all her father cared about. The notorious, fearful Hardy Family.

A tingling in her feet made her legs restless. Was she alone? She couldn't hear the woman any more. Nor whoever she'd been speaking to.

She attempted to move her feet. The tingling had quickly turned into pins and needles and all she wanted was to massage them away. As she tried to move her feet one at a time, the rope, tying her feet together, cut into her young flesh. She called out. "Help!"

It was a feeble attempt. "Help me!" Her voice was strained.

The sound of a door opening and someone shuffling into the room.

"What do you want?" A woman's voice. She carried a strong citrus scent as if she was holding a peeled orange. "Don't make me gag you too!"

Fiona didn't recognise her voice.

"My feet," Fiona said. "Pins and needles."

She felt a hand pull at the rope, trying to loosen it.

"Can you rub them?" It was a strange request, but warranted. "Please."

A sigh. Then she felt soft hands touch her feet. Soothing and steady despite the distinct wobble she had heard in the woman's voice earlier.

I need some warmth. Some kindness.

"Where am I?"

Silence.

Fiona started to sob. "Why are you doing this?"

Still no answer.

Fiona pulled her hands towards her. The chain rattled. She pulled it again, harder and harder. "Help me!" she screamed out. "SOMEBODY HELP!"

"Shush now, be quiet. No one's going to hear you. And no one's going to hurt you either – so long as you behave. Do as you're told. You'll be home before you know it."

The woman had a soft voice and continued to try and keep her calm.

"Here, take some water."

Fiona felt the rim of a cup placed onto her lips, she sipped the moisture.

"Are you hungry?"

Fiona shook her head. "No. I just want to go home."

"Well as soon as your old man coughs up, then you can. But until then . . . "

Fiona scoffed. "Pur-lease! You think my dad's going to hand over money? For me? He'd pay you to take me away more like. My dad couldn't give a toss about me. You should have done your homework."

"Your dad has enough millions. I'm sure he won't miss a few."

"Listen, Lady. I've run away enough times to know. He never comes looking for me. Wanna know his philosophy? To leave me be and I'll come home when I'm ready."

Fiona swallowed. She had never realised how true those words were until she said them out loud. Her relationship with her father was not great. They argued all the time. He would often curse her or tell her to get out of the house and make someone else's life a misery. She started to shake inside.

Daddy Darling! Will you really leave me here to die?

Rewriting the Fairytale

By Karen Leopold Reich

We wet our brushes and dipped into the pans we'd chosen, buttering the bristles with pigment. Not inspired by the colours on offer, I mixed a few together to produce a more evocative shade, and felt myself melting inwardly as I spread it on the paper, luxuriating in the rich, fat, vibrant note of orange. Sometimes that could be so very life-affirming. Sumptuous, sassy, exultant. A glad friend, not your mopey, subtle pastels, shying from engagement like a limp fiancé. This orange was a tonic, energizing, a song to raise a promise to completion. A burst of resolve with a streak of red brawn but without the scrappiness, tempered by bright, larky yellow. Luminous child of the two, orange was a sun-fed soul-lifter, the antidote to self-doubt and wasted opportunity. There was magic to orange. Orange would work.

I surprised myself, as I'd been in thrall to blue for so very long I could scarcely conceive of beauty in any other garb. I was so attuned to blue, my inner wings would flail away at my chest wall when I contemplated the sky's palette of chaste ceruleans, azures, brash cobalts, and dramatic, mystical ultramarine. Yet does the rainbow not instruct us that all colours are wondrous? Every one of its bands is glorious, were one able to separate them out from the infinite range and variation along the spectrum, all significant and all nuance. Like the fabled chakras, they are not in competition with one another, but rather forming a divinely harmonious chord. A marvel when streaking the heavens with reassurance after the rain. How perfectly natural to associate that with the leprechaun's pot of gold, as harmony and balance are the undeniable key to human well-being.

On reflection, since orange was the complement of blue, it might just be I'd dwelt overlong in one ray to the exclusion of others, and this was my instinctive remedy. I was to learn from orange.

Of course, this would have to be a pumpkin with that deep intensity, that was my intuitive sense. Not that it mattered for purposes of the class. We were only meant to convey a quick association, not make any artistic statement.

My hand was already working the brush again to load it full of that delicious potion before reapplying it to the page, and the ridges of a glistening rind were taking shape with each generous padded stroke. Compelling! Then I paused. Not quite your garden variety, this pumpkin, not one to lie low and glow from the ground like some beached, still incandescent, meteorite. This one was already forming a window. This one would have grand golden wheels. This one would have footmen! And its front was already lifting as we departed on a wave length . . .

* * *

I peer from the ripe, lustrous confines of my conveyance, from the satin plush of my seat, frothing and shimmering beneath a cascade of diaphanous silk crinoline. I take in the elegant setting from behind dainty wisps of lace at the window as we proceed spiritedly along the patrician avenue, lanterns blazing, their beams melding into the last sunset rays to keep the horizon burning with expectation. I know about the importance of horizons and thin ribbons of expectation, though surely this, the night of the ball, would rival the firmament in candlepower.

We are approaching the palace now, hooves clapping on the mounting cobblestone drive, a whole bevy of well-turned carriages waiting beyond the portico, light dazzle-spilling from graceful tall windows, splashing the cobblestoned courtyard with brilliance. Countless turrets are set above like a crown upon the royal edifice. The sight stirs a vague and troubling sense of another tower and straw to be spun into gold . . . A stray premonition about all that glitters? About coveting a crown? I recalled my fairy godmother's admonishments and the reminder that I had been allowed to assume this adventure for a purpose.

Magic is a peculiar form of travel. Magic, as the extension of a heart, passes beyond personal lines and those of legend, to the realm of the extra-rational. How else might fantasy be awakened by the kiss of colour on a brush? Fantasy – the boundless pool where ideas and yearnings merge and blend and ripple and piggy-back, where life's sensations are sprinkled and salted and sugared, where time and identity blur. I would come to accept that before the evening was over.

Now, however, we are arriving. A spotlessly gloved hand hovers to help me alight, my gleamingly encased foot meeting the carpet's cushioned weave leading up the broad stone steps, and on through the carved oaken doors, with stories like mine, perhaps, captured on their panels. The vast and lavish vestibule beckons beyond, marble pleated columns standing sentry amidst the immense, starry chandeliers, magnified in splendour by the mirrored galleries.

Attendants receive wraps and nod toward the pearlescent grand staircase. I know these polished twin tiers, curving round and upwards either side, marshalled by the ornately sculpted balustrade to meet at the lip of the great hall's parquet mosaic. I've pictured them so often in my mind's eye, how they part and how they join. Consummation in stone.

The assembled company has already been announced with due pomp and ushered into the main ballroom, where their titters and champagne slide delicately upon pedigree throats. I was not meant to arrive with them, to avoid confusion. Seating plans and dance cards are being consulted, matters of state self-importantly alluded to and deferred to later counsel, as the tides of flounces and bustles sashay past. Military uniforms abound, with lashings of gold braid and ribboned medals on display, high boots at high gloss attention, moustaches and sideburns brandished like trophy pelts before the powdered bouffanterie. Strains of distant chamber strings tease the ear.

I pause, cowed by the spectacle of so much opulence, anxious at the knowledge the step-sisters are there somewhere too, on the most vital of matrimonial crusades. They will not forgive my temerity. They know nothing of fairy godmothers, nor of the wistful flights a deprived woman's fancy can take in the longing by moonlight. I grasp a fold of my gown, sensing convention requires at least the scantiest of curtsies to make an unbidden entrance, and I glance and smile in grateful relief at the fairy glints of rainbow from the crystal bedecked ceiling. A sign. The wheel of the prism is what has brought me back. And magic.

These people, do they think they know me? The question is only fleetingly relevant. In this moment and in this place, I hardly resemble the creature they spurned in their jostling for fortune and position. The sisters notice my arrival, of course, though to them I am just a strange apparition, strangely unaccompanied. So small and fearful of another's advantage they appear now, so intent on being seen in the right circles, obsessed to impress and dispossess.

Others from among the local gentry are intrigued, suspicious. The Queen Mother seeks a bride for her son. Rumour is rife in the kingdom about possible alliances and future campaigns in which any of the multiple dignitaries might relish a role. My foreign regal finery confounds the gathering. Profit, conquest in the air. But this is also the land of other fulfilment.

Before the mincing, fan-quivering matrons can accost me, and probe my credentials, I am gone, claimed by His Majesty the Crown Prince. At last. For this I have braved the journey. The consternation is palpable. As the orchestra launches into the first of many waltzes he sweeps me away, and we whirl and spin, my eyes drinking deep of the glowing invitation in his, my soul thrilling at his touch, and we seem to float on an effervescent current of light, of the like to feed any fairy-tale.

Upon fairy-tale. On and on we reel, locked in that one eternal, transporting moment, merging dream and memory, wish and fable, defying temporal bounds, transcending dutiful vows, on a thread of recaptured delight in unison, soaring, hovering, before gliding gently to rest again at the edge of our stage, where will subsides.

A distant dinner gong sounds, insistent, summoning guests to the banquet. Appetites conflict as curiosity preys, steaming dishes entice, and Her Royal Highness frets that the dawdlers will produce cold soup. The Prince, quietly stiff, now steers me by the arm for a tête-à-tête where the others cannot follow.

Oh, for the delight of once innocent romance. The Prince Charming, the perfect ending. That all the ill fortune, injustice, and hurt might fall away at that instant like feather-down, that true love and devotion might flourish, and the heavens smile on peace and happily-ever-afters!

After so long. Too long. Too long laced by intervening layers of absence.

We resume, but we have slid into a later hue.

A pumpkin fire looms large in the grate and calls my prince to advance. My prince who was, now. I had gazed into those sea-blue eyes with such selfless love, and yet, such diffidence once. I had learned his language, adopted his customs, and slavishly modelled myself after his principles, all for his favour. I had tended to his every need, even prayed to take his fever. I had worshiped him, but the years of dancing now lie in the past, and the passing has been without pledge of troth, without my becoming his queen. Mine has been a sorry exile, though not without the occasional visitation – the dream's descent upon me, in which I am redeemed, reclaimed, and reinstated in his affections, and with such phenomenal force that I rise weak with confusion on waking. And here we are again, in this borrowed space beyond time, beyond waking, enacting the reconciliation.

The Prince is gazing upon me softly, taking my hand dryly in his own. We are not here for the dancing. After studying my face as though to re-memorise my features, he guides me to an elegant settee and invites me to sit with him. He waves away the solicitous manservant as we are, neither of us, hungry for more than this encounter, and fixes his eyes on mine questioningly.

Words slip from him in slow, well-schooled clusters, as he alternates between light jest, conventional enquiry, and appreciation for my coming. He says little about himself other than to present the contours of his current development project, yet plies me with questions about my life. We share pithy comments about the state of the kingdom and the world, we laugh with genuine mirth and pleasure together, though there is the subject we dare not broach. A comfortable, almost conspiratorial sense of intimacy grows like a flame with breath, as the bond we once shared seems somehow still intact. No, we will never be indifferent to one another, not even after all this time. We can be pale kind, pale concerned, pale close.

"You know you have always been very special to me," he insists, almost pleadingly, and the fire flashes on his wedding ring. His voice is disconcertingly high for a man of his stature, the tenor he never became, while I am aware mine has grown stronger and slightly less respectful. Mine is gaining resonance, authority even. I don't return the courtesy. I look on this man and he seems pasty to me after the years in these climes, his eyes now wearing the duller sheen of sea under cloud, his fair hair whitened. The northern latitudes have exacted their toll and chilled his sun, such as ever there was. The aura in which I'd cast him is fading too.

The jealous company beyond the many doors shall perceive nothing. They will not know of this conversation from their future, nor can they speculate about the potential ramifications it might have had. No dramatic changes need be trumpeted.

No, this Cinderella is just a visitor, yet she has had the real treasure in the end, one she would never have known to seek or have hoped to achieve before this night. All that sombre mourning for far too long; too blue, too blue.

I leave this time again, a vague fondness remaining, but with no need to drop a glass slipper.

The clock is striking midnight. The spell has lifted! My Cinderella can depart, having declined the part. Should I have known all those years ago to do so when he failed to see what I saw in marigolds?

Thank you, Fairy Godmother. Thank you magic.

My rainbow has filled out at last, the prize gift of a brushstroke.

This princess is to start a new day in coral self-coronation, the new alchemy accomplished.

And upon a pot of orange gold there sits, not an ashen, sad scruff of a duckling, but a magnificent female swan.

SECRETS

BY ELLEN CARLI

My home is a first-floor flat in a big old house with a beautiful wide staircase. As well as the flat opposite ours, there are two flats downstairs and a room in the attic. When I argue with my older brother, my mother tells us to keep the noise down, or the neighbours will complain and the landlord will throw us out. I don't want that to happen because the house is very special to me.

When I close the heavy front door behind me, I am in heaven. At least, that is what I think heaven looks like. When the light is on, the glass lampshade turns the cream walls into a pale blue sky. I can almost see little winged angels darting around, trying to catch each other.

It makes me feel warm inside to be so close to God. Our Sunday school teacher has told us that God speaks in signs. So, standing in the middle of the hall-heaven, I wait for a sign. One day the light goes off for a second, then comes on again. God has winked at me! I have never thought of God doing things like winking, but it is true. God has definitely winked at me.

I often think about the people who have lived in the house before me and who died of old age, or of some illness. Where are they now? Have their souls really gone to heaven? Do they wear long white gowns and play soft music on harps? Do some people really go to hell? What is it like in hell?

My mother wants me to forget about dead people. "Josephine," she says in her listen-to-me voice that makes me, um, listen. "You're only nine years old, you have your whole life before you. Just be happy and don't worry about what will happen when you get old."

My mother only calls me Josephine, not Josie, when she is cross with me or when she is worried about me. I am not worried about getting old. I just think there must be more exciting things to do than go to school and play with friends.

My mother says I have too much imagination, and my brother calls me a nutcase, but Mr Benson who lives in the attic room, is different. He nods his head when I tell him there are fairies at the bottom of the big neglected garden. He doesn't laugh when I say the cedar tree turns into a wandering long-armed monster at night. He pulls my ponytail and calls me his pretty little angel.

I call him Mr Benson, because my mother says that is the polite thing to do, but he is more like an uncle to me. Not a Dad. I have a Dad, but he lives far away, so I don't see him much. Sometimes I miss him. That's why I like to visit Mr Benson. He makes me laugh, telling silly jokes, just like my Dad. I know Mr Benson is glad to see me, because he lives alone. He has no wife, and no children. He must get lonely sometimes.

My mother thinks Mr Benson is not a good man. "Keep away from him. He can't be trusted," she warns me.

I know why my mother doesn't like Mr Benson. I hear her talk to a friend about two children, a little bit younger than me, who lived nearby, and who have disappeared.

"I bet that man upstairs knows more about it," my mother tells her friend. "I told the police that, and they called him in, but they had to let him go because there was no proof."

I know Mr Benson has done nothing to those little children, but my mother tells her friend she'll find out the truth. "Just wait and see!" she says.

I ask Mr Benson why my mother thinks he can't be trusted. He looks at me with sad eyes. "It's because I look different," he says.

It is true that Mr Benson doesn't look like other men I know. He has a stubbly chin, his clothes are worn, and he always wears a dirty hat, even in the house.

I don't care what Mr Benson looks like, and what other people think of him. He is my friend and the only person who understands me. "When you can't stop thinking about death all the time," he tells me, "the best thing to do is to find out as much about it as you can."

So sometimes, after school, I tell my mother I'm going to play in the garden, but instead I creep up the stairs to Mr Benson's room. He draws the curtains and lights some candles which throw scary shadows on the walls. Then, in the half dark, he tells me tales of delicious happiness or everlasting doom. When I'm frightened, he puts me on his lap and gently strokes my hair. I feel bad about doing things behind my mother's back, but I like to be with Mr. Benson.

Sometimes, we wander around the overgrown garden together, but doing different things. Mr Benson likes to look at birds in the big trees that fill the garden, and I like to look for fairies dancing around pretty toadstools. In some places the bramble bushes are so thick and prickly, they stop you from getting through. Sleeping Beauty's castle must be behind the brambles. She lies in her four-poster bed, waiting for her prince to find her and kiss her awake.

On one of our walks around the garden, I find an old greenhouse hidden under some tall trees. Most of the windows are broken or cracked and the door hangs off one hinge. I call Mr Benson. "Look Mr Benson," I say, "I have my own cottage in the woods. Perhaps Hansel and Gretel will knock on the door, asking for the way home."

Together, we make the cottage into a proper home. In a corner of the garden we find a wonky armchair and a wobbly kitchen table. Mr Benson puts the door back on its hinges and covers the swept floor with an old rug from his room. I borrow an orange table cloth from my mother's kitchen drawer, and I bring some of my books and cuddly toys.

I love my cottage, but I have to make sure my mother doesn't know I'm with Mr Benson. The missing children have still not been found, and everybody thinks somebody must have taken them. My brother tells me lots of people think Mr Benson is the guilty man. I hear people in the shop around the corner talk about him. They say they all know he did it, so why don't the police arrest him? When I hear people talk like that, I run away. I don't want to hear it. It isn't true.

One day, while I am busy in my cottage, Mr Benson comes to visit me. He looks different, but I don't know why. He has his binoculars hanging around his neck, so I know he has been bird watching. Suddenly, I know what is different about him. He isn't wearing his hat. I find out for the first time that he is completely bald. Perhaps that is why he always wears a hat.

He also has a nasty scratch on his face. Mr Benson explains that when looking at a bird, he tried to get past an overgrown rose bush which scratched his face and took his hat. He points at a tall rosebush which has a hat dangling from a branch. "Have you ever seen such a strange rose?" he jokes. Then he looks serious, almost frightened. "Promise me something," he says, lifting my chin with one finger so that I have to look at him. "Promise me that if you see or find something strange in the garden, you'll tell me first."

I nod my head. Of course I'll promise. After all, he is the only person I share secrets with. Mr Benson looks relieved. Then he leaves, forgetting to take his hat.

I stay on for a while but when I notice it is beginning to get dark, I am in a hurry to get home. When I'm late, my mother starts looking for me, and I don't want her to find my cottage in the woods.

On my way back to the big house I hear a scraping noise at the edge of the garden. It must be a fox. Mr Benson has told me that foxes stay in their holes under the ground during the day and come out looking for food at night. When I creep slowly forward towards the noise, I see not a fox but a man. His blond hair lights up in the half darkness. He wears jeans, a blue jacket and white trainers. He holds a spade which he hides behind some bramble bushes. Then he climbs over the garden wall and disappears.

What is going on? Who is this man, and what is he doing in our garden? What has he used the spade for, and why doesn't he go out of the garden through the gate in front of the house instead of climbing over the wall?

I have never seen the man before, and he has scared me. In my hurry to turn around, I stumble, and when I put my hand down to stop myself from falling, I feel something hard. In a panic, I grab the thing and run, but I slow down when the lights of the house can be seen. Only then do I look at what I have in my hand. It's a small shoe covered in mud.

When I get inside the house, I run upstairs to Mr Benson's room to show him what I have found, but he is not in. In our flat my mother is waiting for me. She wants to know what I'm hiding behind my back. I don't want to talk to her before I have seen Mr Benson, but she goes on so much, I have to show her, and tell her where it comes from.

My mother looks very serious, and sends me to my room. After a while some policemen arrive. They set up strong lights in the garden, and start looking at the ground they walk on. The policemen find something, but they refuse to say more. My brother tells me all this. I'm not allowed out of the house.

My brother thinks the police have found the missing children. "Mr Benson is as guilty as hell," he says. "He will go to prison for a long time."

I don't understand what he is talking about. The children have been found, so Mr Benson has done nothing. Perhaps they made a den in our garden, and were hiding there. "What is Mr Benson guilty of?" I ask, but my brother doesn't answer.

A policeman comes to our flat holding a hat in a plastic bag.

"That's Mr Benson's hat!" I tell him helpfully.

My mother and the policeman take me into our living room where he asks me lots of questions. "Did you visit Mr Benson in his room?" "What did you do there?" "What did Mr Benson do?"

I don't mind the policeman knowing that Mr Benson is my friend. So I tell him how kind Mr Benson is. How he tells me stories about life after death and sits me on his lap when I'm upset. But I say nothing about what I have seen in the garden. That is my secret until I can tell Mr Benson about it.

My mother hugs me tight. "You could have been next," she says. Next for what? I want to ask, but I know this is not the right time. "Don't you worry," my mother goes on. "That man will get his just desserts."

I hope it will be apple pie. Mr Benson loves apple pie.

A policeman stands guard outside Mr Benson's room, waiting for him to get back. Looking through the net curtains in our living room I watch Mr Benson get into a police car. I want to shout at him, say nice things to him, but the words won't come.

Later, burying my face in my pillow, and thinking about Mr Benson locked up in a cell, with only bread to eat and water to drink, I cry myself to sleep.

Now I can never tell Mr Benson about the blond man in the garden and the spade hidden behind the thick bramble bushes.

She Lay Where She Would Lie

By Karen Leopold Reich

She lay where she would lie
Till the next high tide,
Orange sun-daubed bill
Frozen in profile, still,
Feathers splayed
Colour-side down,
Across the proud mound of seaweed.
Like a wingspread Egyptian deity,
She lies in state,
Sightless, flightless
To our eyes,
And I pay my respects to her
Gravity-shorn spirit,
While lacy waves dimple darkly
Beyond the sand,
And the wailers slide high on the wind
Announcing the burial at sea.

The Constant Inspector

By Mary Gumsley

Inspector Cliff Evans lit up a cigarette as he paused to look down on the Canterbury University Car Park for what seemed to him to be the millionth time in fifteen years. Occasionally he felt that he spent more time at the University than at his office in the Police Station.

However, with two unsolved murder cases dating back to fifteen years ago on the same University campus, it was important to find a solution.

Stinging cigarette smoke blew in his eyes as he peered at endless rows of motor bikes and cars of all descriptions.

Neither the car park nor the students using it had changed much. They chose to park their vehicles in the same spot every day if they could. That should have made his job easier, but if you don't know what you are looking for, then nothing is simple.

He thought back over the unsolved cases: two female students had been murdered, a third had escaped with severe injuries. She had heard a motor bike starting up just before passing out.

An unused orange handkerchief had been found at the crime scene, but forensics had failed to identify the DNA on the item.

Inspector Evans climbed the stairs to see the caretaker, who had been seen near the crime scene. His grandson, who had been staying with him at the time, had provided an alibi.

The Inspector was due to retire in two years, and he wanted a solution. He did not want to be haunted by failures in his older years. He knocked firmly on the caretaker's door. The two old men knew each other well. The caretaker knew what to expect when the Inspector came knocking, and always offered him tea and biscuits.

The ritual was observed, and they were both seated when Cliff Evans heard a sudden roar from the kitchen.

"Just the washing machine," sighed Alan. "Got me grandson staying with me again. Remember him? Couldn't hold down a job."

Inspector Evans did remember him; a spotty, ginger-haired youth with stained clothes, not at all the type to mix with University students.

"Well, he has a job for the moment," continued Alan, "but I still worry about his future. What if he carries on cruising around aimlessly, disappearing when he feels like it, like he has done so often in the past?" Then he stopped as if he remembered something.

The machine went into a loud spin in the kitchen and the old man went in to check on it. The inspector followed him, watching as he bent over to remove the clothes. As the Inspector could see that Alan was now going to be busy, he decided to take his leave. As he turned round, he suddenly glimpsed something extremely colourful amongst the washing. He thought it must be something belonging to the grandson. Alan seemed to wear just blue uniform and blue accessories, even off duty.

He walked slowly to his car thinking he was going to have to accept his failure, when something registered in his mind about the grandson. He and Alan had discussed cruising around. Criminals often cruise around, and disappear occasionally in an erratic fashion; it is part and parcel of their 'business'. Alarm bells started to ring in his mind. Then he thought about the colourful item. Was it a handkerchief?

His heart skipped a beat. He also had a feeling the grandson owned a motor bike. Perhaps it was a moped? He couldn't remember.

He knew he had to speak to him immediately, so he raced up the stairs, almost tripping over in his haste to get to the flat. He knocked loudly and repeatedly on the door. From inside, Alan shouted "Stop that! The whole neighbourhood can hear you! I'm coming!"

Evans' jaw tightened as he waited for the old man to open the door.

A lengthy silence prevailed as the Inspector glanced down at the orange handkerchief in Alan's hand, then stared at the caretaker. He realised that Alan had always known his grandson was guilty of those crimes, and had been lying to him for more than fifteen years.

THE DUTIFUL SON

BY ELLEN CARLI

They were my next-door neighbours in an unfashionable part of London. There was Hussain, over six-feet tall and handsome, Saira, his petite wife, and their four well-behaved children aged between ten and three years. We were strange bedfellows; an unsophisticated young couple from a former colony, and a well-educated, middle-class English woman at least twenty years their senior.

Saira gave me no more than a shy nod each time we saw each other. Hussain usually said 'Hello,' but he did not stop to remark on the weather or whatever seemed appropriate. The phrase 'They keep themselves to themselves' certainly applied to them.

As an increasing number of immigrants from the other side of the world moved into the neighbourhood, I watched its character change. Newly-opened shops sold brightly coloured saris, ornaments from the Indian continent, foreign spices and exotic-looking vegetables I had never seen before. I felt like an outsider. My sense of exclusion created a wall between my neighbours and me. I, too, kept myself to myself.

Then, one fine spring morning, I was late for my train, so I decided to drive to work in my bright orange Volkswagen Beetle, a relic from my hippy days. To my horror the old banger failed to start. I was desperate. I managed to open the bonnet to reveal the engine, but that was it.

I was still pondering what to do when Hussain happened to come out of his house. I fully expected him to walk straight past me and my bothersome motor, but he stopped and offered to take a look. Within minutes the engine was ticking over nicely. I thanked him, complimenting him for his familiarity with car engines. Hussain shrugged. "It's my job," he said, "I'm a car mechanic." It was the first time I heard him utter more than one word.

After this ice-breaking encounter Hussain proved himself to be anything but unsociable. He came to my rescue several times when my ageing Beetle gave up the ghost. He gave me lifts to the station, and to the shops. He drove me to A&E when I nearly lost a finger trying to cut a frozen piece of meat in half. He patiently waited while I was treated, then took me home again.

During these rides I was given glimpses of Hussain's background. He was born in rural Pakistan, but his parents left for England when he was eight years old. Hussain was silent for a few moments, scratching first his head and then the bridge of his nose, before saying softly, "It was a difficult time for me, especially in school."

I saw the scene before me. Quiet, polite, diligent Hussain was a pleasure to have in the classroom. 'Teacher's pet' other children called him. It made him a prime target for bullies but he didn't help himself by shyly walking away instead of facing them head on. Shouts of 'cowardy, cowardy custard,' and 'Paki,' followed him all the way home.

He learned to speak English fairly quickly, but he struggled with the three Rs. When he left school without qualifications he was lucky to get a job in his uncle's clothing factory where he soon became known as a conscientious worker who could go far.

At the age of nineteen he went back to Pakistan to marry his cousin Saira. They had not seen each other for a decade, but their respective parents agreed they were a good match.

Then, suddenly, Hussain clammed up, staring grimly at the road ahead. I tried to continue the conversation.

"Where did you and Saira live in England?"

"With my parents."

The short, sharp tone warned me not to trespass. We ended the journey in uneasy silence.

The subject was never broached again, but a few months later I had an opportunity to return Hussain's kindness. Giving me a lift to the station, he told me Saira had to go into hospital for a minor operation, leaving him to juggle his job with the care of his children.

I knew enough about families of Hussain's background to wonder why nobody ever came to visit my neighbours. Family ties were important to them, so his relatives would undoubtedly have helped him out while Saira was in hospital. I suspected something was wrong, but I knew better than to ask.

I offered to collect the children from school and take them home with me. Hussain hesitated, not wanting to impose, but eventually he thankfully agreed. After being fed, the children were happily watching a film on television when Hussain came to collect them, bringing me a curry Saira had cooked and kept in the freezer. As I expected, my suggestion to share the food between us was first rejected but, after some insistence, accepted.

We sat at the kitchen table eating, when, out of the blue, Hussain began to talk about himself. It was as if he had finally decided to confide in me.

"After we got married we lived with my parents," he said, starting with the answer to the question I had asked him several months ago. "Everything was fine. Saira helped my mother keep the house clean, cook, wash our clothes. She worked hard and my mother was pleased with her."

Hussain paused for a moment, staring sadly into the distance. Nobody could have foreseen what happened next. Saira's parents claimed they could not afford the dowry they had promised, as was customary in their community. Her in-laws were furious. They refused any pay delay, or debt reduction. Honour was at stake; compromises were out of the question.

After several angry exchanges by telephone and letter, Hussain's parents decided enough was enough. Their son was ordered to divorce Saira who was four months pregnant. She would be sent back to her parents in disgrace.

Then the unthinkable happened. Mild-mannered, compliant Hussain refused to give in to his parents' demand.

"Saira had done nothing wrong," he told me. "She was a good wife. I had no reason to divorce her."

Hussain's parents soon realised that any amount of persuasion and bullying had no effect. Next, they tried to drive Saira out. Hussain's mother made her work harder and longer hours than before. She criticised everything Saira did, calling her a bad wife, not good enough for her son.

When nothing seemed to work, the couple were told to leave. At the same time Hussain's uncle fired him from his job. The family closed ranks against him. Hussain and Saira were ostracised.

Hussain cleared his throat before continuing. "I looked for work everywhere," he said softly. "All I could find was a job in an Indian restaurant doing the washing up."

They moved into a run-down house with dangerously rotten stairs. Their damp room was so dark, the light had to be left on for most of the day. It was a miserable environment for a couple expecting their first child, but it was all they could afford.

After the arrival of their daughter, Saira suffered a severe bout of depression. The doctor told Hussain that it could have been caused by the birth and aggravated by their living conditions.

"Saira did her best," Hussain said in his gentle manner, "but she was too depressed to feed Nadia properly. The baby lost a lot of weight. In the end they were both admitted to hospital."

Good physical and medical care did wonders for mother and child, but not long after they were discharged, the young couple were dealt the cruellest blow of all. Hussain winced at the painful memory.

"When I came home from work one day, they had both gone." Hussain paused, thoughtfully examining his clean but grease-ingrained mechanic's hands. "I knew something was wrong," he went on. "Saira never left the room without me. I looked in the wardrobe and saw that their clothes had gone."

Hussain realised immediately what had happened. He ran all the way to his parents' house where he banged loudly on the closed door. "I know you have Saira," he shouted, "I want her back!"

Eventually the door opened just wide enough for Hussain's father to show his face, "What do you want?"

"I want Saira. I know you have taken her."

"She is not here."

Hussain knew there was no time to waste with angry exchanges. He ran to the nearest telephone box (mobiles were still rare) and dialled 999. Fortunately, the police officer he spoke to believed his story. The police intervention came just in time; Saira and the baby were found at Heathrow airport, awaiting a flight to Karachi, escorted by Hussain's cousin who used to be his childhood playmate.

I stared at Hussain, unable to find words that could express my feelings of anger on his behalf. 'Sorry' would sound inadequate. Instead I said, "I hope you filed a complaint with the police."

Hussain gave me an apologetic smile. "I didn't. After all, they are family."

Now I was speechless. His family had deliberately made him homeless and penniless, but Hussain had refused to charge them with the kidnap of his wife and child. Yet, instead of rallying around this brave and loyal young man, they could not forgive his disobedience. As punishment, Hussain and Saira were shunned for ever.

In the mean time, Hussain's search for better work paid off as he was offered an apprenticeship with a local garage. He worked hard to learn as much as he could, and his efforts were rewarded with a full-time job. The couple moved to a flat where Saira was much happier. The arrival of more children prompted them to buy a house, so becoming my neighbours.

Hussain paused for a few seconds, still staring at his hands. "What I regret most," he said, his voice trembling slightly, "Is that my children have never met their grandparents who live not far away. I have tried many times, but they refuse to see us."

I was ready to give him my opinion of his spiteful family, but it appeared Hussain had not finished his dramatic story. His head bowed, as if to shield himself from my sharp tongue, he said, "My parents are getting old now. I am their only son. I have a duty to look after them."

A whirlwind of questions and thoughts went around in my head. Was this man for real? What kind of person can even think of caring for his parents after they treated him so badly? I was ready to give him my thoughts of his selfish family. It was *my* duty to stop him mollycoddling his undeserving relatives. Before I opened my mouth, I glanced at Hussain. He looked at peace with himself. The calm expression on his face made me see matters in a different light. I understood, as if in a flash, that the society he had been born into functioned through unbreakable rules and duties. They often brought harmony, but sometimes they caused friction and even hostility.

Hussain knew he had broken an important rule by disobeying his parents in order to remain loyal to his wife. In his eyes – no matter how painful their responses had been for him – his family had not acted inappropriately. There was nothing to hate them for.

The anger I had felt inside me drained away slowly. I realised that my young friend was comfortable with his cultural demands. Although my western upbringing made me disapprove of the causes of his family's feud, Hussain had accepted them. What right did I have to disturb his inner peace?

I stood up from my chair and uttered the phrase generations of English people have used to express sympathy. I said: "Would you like a cup of tea?"

THE GALLERY

BY SARAH MEAKINS

The car screeched to a halt and Amy leapt out, bright orange handbag flying behind her. She was late again! *One of these days*, she thought, *I'll arrive on time, looking neat, tidy and demure instead of out of breath and like a spider on skates.*

Amy's artwork was being displayed in the prestigious new gallery in town, and she should have been there half an hour ago for a 'meet the artist' session. Everything had gone against her that morning; her hair had decided to pick this day to defy gravity, sticking out at impossible angles, and the sunset orange top that had seemed so nice in the shop did not go with anything else, especially not the 'matching' bag and shoes.

Amy, cheeks glowing with a mixture of embarrassment and exhaustion, pushed opened the door and approached the reception desk.

"Hello, I'm Amy Grimsley. I'm here for the viewing of my painting – a bit late – sorry!" Amy spurted out.

"Ok, let me see," said the receptionist, typing in a few details. "Yes, that was supposed to be at 10.30."

"I know. I'm running late – I might have mentioned that."

"Well, it's in the Lilac Room. Go straight ahead, through the double doors, up the stairs, turn right, sharp left, second room on your right. They may have finished by now though. There's an *important* artist, I obviously can't disclose details, coming in very shortly and we need to make sure it's just right for him. Thank you." The receptionist turned in a deliberate manner and tapped away on the keyboard.

Feeling well and truly put in her place, Amy tried to follow the instructions, but having the memory of a goldfish didn't help. She got as far as the top of the stairs. This place is massive, she thought, glancing at 'Stag Night', a fascinating sculpture of a moon trapped in antlers, which had been positioned at the entrance to the first floor. *Now, right or left? Definitely left, my memory's not that bad!*

Hurrying down the corridor, she had to retrace her steps when she realised that there was only one doorway on each side of it. *Just as well this isn't the National,* she laughed to herself, *or I'd never find my picture!* After going to almost every other room in the gallery, she eventually found the Lilac Room.

They've done this up very nicely, she thought, looking at the decorated tables full of drinks and posh nibbles. *They said there might be a free cuppa in it, but this looks very smart.* Amy hurried past a couple gazing at a portrait and tried to locate her masterpiece. Surrounded by all these stunning paintings, sculptures and installations, she was feeling rather nervous about her piece now. Her friends had told her how fantastic it was, that the gallery was having a competition and she should exhibit. Now, with the proper works of art all around, she couldn't believe that she had managed to win. Her watercolour, entitled 'Oranges Are Not The Only Fruit But They Are My Favourite' was judged as being 'unusual', 'distinctive', and 'fresh – a pleasant change'.

There were a few people admiring a painting which was the focus of the display. Under the picture was a large label: 'Amy Grimsley, Competition Winner'. Overwhelmed with confusion, she took a second glance; it wasn't her painting. What was going on? Where was it? She turned, looking for an attendant, and bumped into the person next to her.

"Sorry!" she squeaked.

"Sorry!" he echoed.

Staring back at her was Jack Swanley, former male model turned Manoir art prize winner, one of the judges of the competition, and her inspiration.

"They've got the wrong painting," she uttered in a bewildered state, gesturing towards the display.

"Yes, they have." He seemed equally confused as he peered at the picture.

"That's not my painting! It's not mine! What's going on?"

"No, it's mine. It obviously shouldn't be there!"

With them both gesticulating wildly, Sonia, the attendant, rushed over to see what the fuss was about.

"Can I help you?"

"Yes, you can!" Jack exclaimed "That's not her painting, it's mine!"

"If you'd both like to come over here a moment, I'm sure we can sort this out," she said, desperately trying to be professional and not show quite how nervous she was.

Sonia led them into a side room, and offered them a seat. She then phoned her manager who could be heard indistinctly on the other end.

"The manager will be straight up. I'm so sorry for the mix up," she informed them.

"But where's my picture?" Amy cried.

"That's what we're going to find out." Sonia smiled awkwardly. Her radio buzzed, causing her to apologise profusely and scuttle out of the room.

"Well, this is different!" said Jack, smiling and breaking the silence.

"If I'd been on time, we could have sorted this out before everyone turned up," Amy wailed.

"I'm sure it will all turn out alright." He paused. "You must be Amy Grimsley then? I loved your work. So original."

"Thank you," Amy responded, uncertain how to reply to praise from the great Jack Swanley.

At that moment, the manager appeared, wringing her hands and fawning apologetically over Jack.

"I'm so, so sorry! Please accept my humble and profuse apologies!" she flustered, almost bowing as she spoke. "We have located Ms Grimsley's piece. I'm afraid it was being displayed under your name, sir." Cue more bowing and hand wringing.

"No harm done then." He beamed. "When you've put them right, I'd like to introduce Ms Grimsley to my agent, if that's OK with her. After all, they've done wonders for me and I'd love for your work to get more publicity," he said, smiling at Amy.

"Wow! Yes please! I'll have to be late more often," she exclaimed, hugging him with excitement, before quickly releasing him, apologising and turning crimson with embarrassment, despite Jack's reassurances. It was just the thought of having her own agent. Amy hadn't allowed herself to even dream of that.

"Do you want to grab a coffee from the café downstairs while we wait for them to sort it all out? I hear they do a mean lemon drizzle cake too. It beats the dried-out sandwiches they've got next door!" Jack offered, laughing.

"That would be great!" Amy squeaked, trying hard to take in the whole situation.

He chuckled as he and Amy linked arms and swept out of the room giggling together, leaving Sonia and her snooty manager staring after them.

THE LAST DANCE

BY SUSAN EMM

Orange bruise in sky
Kicked from heels of tango shoes
The last dance of day.

THE PRICE OF LOVE

BY KIM HAMMOND

The most stunning girl in school strolled into the dining hall. Meghan Jones. I tried not to stare. Instead I kept my head down, hoped she wouldn't see me, and carried on munching on my cheese toasty.

She walked towards me, dropped a piece of folded orange paper into my lap, and turned away. Not before smiling though. A slow suggestive smile that would get most guys in Year Ten excited.

I smiled back awkwardly, at the same time breathing a sigh of relief that she wasn't stopping, nearly choking on a slab of melted Mozzarella cheese that wasn't sure which tube it should slide down. As she walked away from me, she shook her head sexily, whipping her long hair from side to side. I tried to concentrate on my sandwich but I watched as, two rows in front of me, she pulled out a chair, turned, gave me an 'I know you think I'm cute look', and sat down.

I carefully unpicked the note that had been folded into eight and read, 'Fancy a date? Meet me behind the gym block after school.'

My pulse raced in the back of my throat. One of the most attractive girls in our year group had just asked me out and here I was wishing she hadn't.

All the boys in my form thought Meghan Jones was gorgeous. None more so than my best friend Garth. He'd asked her out only last week, but she'd said no. If I had felt bad for him then, I felt worse for him now. Now, she'd just asked me out. How did I tell him that? The last thing we needed was some girl messing up our friendship.

I hated lying to Garth. He'd been my best friend since Year One. I was new to the school, having just moved into the area two weeks before, and Garth had been given the job of being my Buddy. I remember that first day clearly. We'd gone on a class outing, foraging in the forest. We'd found a frog amongst the leaves and Garth hid it inside his jumper. When we'd got back to school he let it loose into the classroom. When Miss Jessop, our teacher, saw it, she screamed and jumped on top of a table. Miss Jessop refused to come down until Mr Berwick, the head, caught the frog and took it back to the forest. It was proper hysterical. Although Miss Jessop didn't think so. She kept us both in at playtime.

"Budge up," Garth said, sliding into the chair next to me. He eyed the piece of paper I was turning in my hand and snatched at it. "Is that a love letter?"

"It's nothing," I said, hastily slipping it into the inside pocket of my blazer. I looked Garth straight in his eyes. Suddenly I felt sick.

"Go on mate," Garth shoved me, "who's it from?"

I knew Garth would be devastated if he found out Meghan had just asked me out. The thought of meeting her after school made my mouth dry. My voice, that hadn't quite broken yet, suddenly shrilled, "It's just a letter from my mum to get me out of football practice."

More lies.

I felt droplets of sweat gather across my forehead at the thought of being alone with Meghan. I had never been any good at speaking to girls. I even struggled to talk to boys.

"Hmmm." Garth flicked his floppy fringe out of his blue eyes. Ever since he had turned fifteen, he'd rapidly morphed into a man. His face had lost its chubbiness and had become more chiselled, his jaw line more defined. The day Garth had started to notice girls, he'd also started to eat healthily, and took up weight lifting. He was looking proper buff.

Meghan Jones choosing me over Garth made no sense at all.

But then what I did next made no sense either.

As Garth took a bite into his meat sandwich, I pushed my toasty to one side. I didn't feel hungry any more.

Meghan looked back at me then. I shifted uneasily in my seat and clocked Garth ogling her up and down.

Garth smiled at Meghan and she smiled back. But not at him. It was clearly me she was smiling at.

"Did you see that mate?" Garth whispered. He grabbed my arm and squeezed it.

"See what?" I pulled my arm away. It irritated me the way he drooled over Meghan. I wanted to shout, "You're wasting your time, Mate. It's actually ME she likes, not you."

But I couldn't.

I thought the world of Garth. But he was clearly in love with Meghan. Should I tell him the truth? About my feelings? About Meghan's? Would he understand, if I did? I couldn't bear to lose his friendship.

"Look at her, mate. She's like drooling over me. D'ya reckon she's changed her mind about going out with me?" The hope in Garth's voice was unmistakable. His breathing changed, it was deeper, faster.

That was when I lost it.

The plot, I mean. Really lost it.

Shaking inside, I pulled the note out of my pocket and threw it at him. "Changed her mind? What do you think?" My blood felt as though it was swelling, getting hot under my skin. I'd just put nine years of friendship at risk. There was no going back.

Garth read the note, then he folded it and gave it back to me. We sat in stillness, neither one of us speaking for what seemed like ages. The dining hall emptied, until eventually there was just me and Garth and a couple of Year Sevens. I hadn't even noticed Meghan leave.

Garth spoke first, "You interested in her?"

My stomach turned over as I thought about what I was about to say – what I was about to do – to Garth, my best friend. I couldn't hide my emotions any longer. I had to tell him the truth. Even if telling the truth meant losing my best friend.

Before I could speak, Garth leapt out of his seat and towered over me. "You are interested in her, aren't you? I thought you were my *friend*," he yelled at me.

"I am your friend," I screeched back. "And I'm not interested." I swallowed hard. "Not in her anyway."

Garth's stern gaze softened. He asked, "Then who?"

"You – Garth – I love you."

Garth hasn't spoken to me since that day last week in the dining room. In fact, a few of the kids in school give me a wide berth now. But that's okay. Yes, Garth was a huge part of my life, but hiding something so vital from him was wearing me down. It probably sounds corny, but as much as I miss Garth's friendship, I'm much happier now, being myself. My form teacher, Mr Shepard, told me there are lots of other boys out there like me. I just gotta get out there and meet them. And I will, one day.

When I'm over Garth.

The Problems With Modern Technology

by Tracey Jacobs

'Orange Is the New Black.' Teenagers and lots of other people have all seen this on Netflix! What on earth is Netflix? the old man thought. He threw the magazine onto the sofa and chuckled with a confused look on his face, as he tried yet again to get his head around modern technology. "Honestly," he said out loud, "in my day we had a box on the wall, and you had to get up and change it to a different channel if you wanted to watch another programme. A, B, C, D, or E – they were your choices. Oh, and there was an F, I think. If you missed one, too bad. No way of seeing it unless they showed it again. I wonder what 'Orange Is the New Black' is about, and why it's not on the telly?" he sighed.

Terry was seventy-eight, and had personally had enough of all these modern gadgets. He would say you just learn one thing and they bring out a new version of it. Either that or it packs up completely! "In my day if you bought something, you bought it to last," he said.

Now, I was very proud of myself, he thought, *when I mastered the video recorder. That was your first chance to be out and about without worrying about being back home for your favourite programmes.* Chuckling to himself, he remembered how easily he understood all the instructions that came with them. *Oh, and then what? They change* those and it's a DVD player and you can get all the things from yesteryear that we rushed home to watch! 'The Avengers', 'Man in a Suitcase', and all the England football matches. You can get them all in HMV and other stores now. Blimey, takes me back a good few years!

Now, back to my mobile, he sat staring at it, why is it called an orange one, when it's black? Weird! Someone earlier was talking about a blackberry, I just don't get it. The youngsters of today whizz through all these things and understand it all and I don't. Sometimes I feel very silly, but I manage to make a joke out of it. Sim cards. Talk-time? That was a work break in my day, the time to catch up with everyone. Now, they all have the latest mobile right by their side as they work. Unusual if you ask me. Well, no one is asking me are they? Again, he laughed quietly to himself, remembering the time when he thought he would make an effort to get fitter, so he took a slow (and I mean slow) walk to the park. He noticed that all the teenagers seemed to have hearing aids, which made his daughter go into fits of giggles as he accused parents of letting their children go deaf through so much loud music.

"Oh my God, Dad," she'd laughed, "They're earphones. They're listening to their music as they walk." He did feel silly. On some occasions, he got so bored with his own company he rang the speaking clock. At least he knew how to do that. Must remember to hang up, though!

Terry sat for a while and thought about calling his daughter, but each time he tried she would say to him later "Dad, I got a very long voicemail from you, with nothing on it. I could hear you bustling about." Now that's a confusing one, if you ask me. If I haven't left a message, what does she hear? Then he remembered the time when his brother had run around to the phone box to call an ambulance when Sylvie had gone into labour with their first child. Now, of course, they'd use a mobile.

He sat thinking for a while about how things had changed over the years. Some things were obviously for the best. Medically, things were better, and it was quicker to get anything now – no Sunday closing for the shops. Some changes had improved life for the many. On the other hand, it seemed unfair that some people had this attitude that the elderly knew nothing. He hated it when people showed him things that he didn't understand because there had been a time when he understood almost everything.

I need to do a modern technology course, he thought, *learn all about these computer things and how to do everything online now. Yes, that's it. I'll go along and have professional guidance, then I can't go wrong, can I? I can get one of those tablet things that they're all going on about, stupid name for a device – but it shouldn't give me a headache, should it?* he grinned, but then he sat on the remote control and it went haywire. "Oh, bugger it," he said impatiently, "now how do I get back to 'Homes Under the Hammer'?"

Terry started dozing. Some wildlife programme was on, he hadn't got a clue what he was watching and it was very loud. Post came through the door and with that he came back into the world of the living, slowly getting up to look at today's correspondence. *Ah the bank,* he smiled, *think that's my new pin number.* He tore open the envelope and looked everywhere for this number but it wasn't clearly displayed. "Blimey, how am I supposed to find it?" he asked himself, "all this gumf! I only asked for a new card and I get all this." With that he decided he needed to speak to one of his girls. "Ah, they'll know," he said, smiling.

Terry phoned his daughter (from the landline of course) as she would know all about this card business. "I'll call in later Dad," she said. "It's simple enough." *Mmm,* he thought, *it may be simple to you but it baffles me no end.* He could relax now though, someone who understands was coming soon.

I don't know, Terry thought, *Sky TV, remote controls, money coming out of walls, things that give you directions in your car! Not sure if I will ever get used to it. Microchips, now they were the first ever chips to be cooked in a microwave weren't they? Now they tell me no way, behave! But I really thought that,* he remembered. *Microwave oven cooking chips, a microchip surely!* He laughed softly: *And a mouse to eat the bits that go on the floor obviously! Maybe a long piece of wire is its tail,* he joked.

Would he ever master the art of modern technology? He learned to drive buses and cars years ago, not forgetting the four times he went out to Australia and had flying lessons. In his younger years, he'd shovelled tons of coal daily, and delivered it to all the houses. Then for about ten years he was a paint sprayer in a small garage, which kept his head above water for paying the bills and mortgage. He had never been unemployed. Never! His CV would look out of date now, but let's be honest here, his skills were those that were necessary for the time. Would he even know what a CV was? If he'd ever needed one, he didn't need it now.

Modern technology might be confusing to understand, but don't forget that there's always been an earlier version of things. During WW2, there were no photocopiers or typewriters that had memories, and they coped with what they had to do, with the technology that was available then. Telephone boxes were on every corner *and* they were kept in good working order. Not many people had their own private phone at home. The art of conversation was lost, everything done by social media and messaging now, so in some ways things were easier back then. But still, they'd had their challenges.

Later, Terry's daughter arrived and explained all about the bank and the PIN. He was under strict instructions never to give this four-digit number to anyone – even she didn't want to see it. She found it all in the corner of this long letter and peeled it off carefully. Trouble is, he said it out loud, "Four-three-two-eight it says, is that right?" She fell about laughing, it was just hilarious to watch, and once again he felt a fool. At least she had seen the funny side!

He then went on to tell her he was seriously thinking about learning a bit more to do with computers and stuff as he had the time now. When he asked how he would find out about a technology course, laughter again, as all the details are online.

Oh well, he thought, *if you can laugh at yourself, you can achieve anything, but I will get to watch that 'Orange Is the New Black'.*

THE STORY OF BANJO PATTERSON – THE MAN FROM ORANGE

BY DAVID MORRISH

I was born in Orange, a dusty little town in New South Wales (NSW) near the outback, six hours north-west of Sydney. In the middle of 'nowhere' really, unless you count the 'darkest skies capital' of Coonemerara, home to the most important astronomical observatory in Australia.

The old back route through Orange was frequented by outlaws and crooks. NSW used to be more lawless than the Wild West, until a colonial police force was set up to catch, tame – and usually hang – the bushwhackers. Orange was, and still is a fruit-growing town, producing apples, pears and even grapes. Paradoxically, almost every fruit but oranges! Despite its warmth, it's not quite warm enough for such exotic fruit. People constantly taunt locals (some "take the pith" out of us) about the absence of actual oranges from the fruit-growing town of Orange.

In the early days of European settlement, the continent had to be reached and opened up, not just via a long sailing-ship voyage from Europe, down the Atlantic, and across the Indian Ocean, but by coastal craft along its extensive coastline.

Cross-country distances between cities were, and are, vast. Before the days of air travel, the fractured eastern coast was a monstrous obstacle even to railway travel. It took twelve days to sail from Sydney to the port of Darwin. The Federation of Australia was only made a reality by the construction of a rail bridge in 1889 across the mighty Hawksbury River, twenty-five kilometres north of Sydney. That simple, but expensive bridge cut the train travel time between the cities of Sydney and Brisbane in half.

It's hard to understand what life must have been like in Victorian times without appreciating that the State is nearly four times the size of the UK and almost equivalent to France and Germany combined. Most of the state to the west of the Blue Mountains was cut off from Sydney's civilisation, making policing almost impossible so NSW was much wilder in the 1880's than the USA's western frontier – that's why Butch Cassidy wanted to go there! These days, the only glimpse Sydney's citizens have of the great outback is at the Olympic Park when the city hosts the Easter Agricultural Show. This brings farmers, cowboys and "hillbillies" to the city, along with their plethora of produce and livestock, and events such as sheep shearing, rodeo, and timber chopping contests.

Although I eventually gained a (false) reputation as a 'bushie' and roustabout, I was born into a respectable down-to-earth farming family, who christened me Andrew Barton Patterson. My old man was a dour Scot who migrated early in the 1840's. Soon after my birth, our family moved to an isolated station near the Snowy Mountains. When I was five, my father lost his wool clip in a flood and was forced to sell up. Fortunately for us, my uncle died not long after, so dad returned to Orange to take over uncle's farm, close to the only route between Melbourne and Queensland.

Taking over uncle's farm created a good life for my folks, and my father became a respectable farmer. So much so that he was intent, it seemed, on trying to make me into a gentleman from an early age. I guess he kind of failed. Being brought up in the country, on the route between Melbourne and Sydney, bullock teams, stage coaches, and drovers were familiar sights to me. We also saw horsemen from the Snowy Mountains country taking part in picnic races and polo matches. I learnt to ride and love horses early on – a love that stayed with me all my life, and became an inspiration for my early writing.

Dad sent me off to become 'civilised' as he put it. I lived with Granny in the City, and he paid for me to be educated at a Grammar School in Sydney. He wanted me to be a lawyer, of all things! But I was always a bit of a dreamer, a drifter and a 'larrikin'. I revelled in telling stories and writing songs. I especially loved horses, and even played polo – which, between you and me, I was bloody good at. What would you expect? I'd been brought up in the saddle back in Orange, so chasing a little ball around with a pack of jolly boys was easy, after learning with real cattlemen roughriders. Throughout my life, horses and horse-riding remained my passion! Nevertheless, my old man was delighted when I eventually left school and trained to become a solicitor.

BP was an incorrigible addict to horse riding and racing, and in latter years he edited a Racing Paper. Gambling is still far more prevalent in Australia than in UK or Europe. The racing coverage in the Aussie press is far greater than in British newspapers. These days most pubs have a betting desk. But very rare indeed are the picturesque pubs, pictured in "Beer Adverts" and tourist posters. The majority of urban pubs in NSW are grim – squalid hybrids of cheap bar, pokie (fruit machine) room, and bookie counter, frequented by lowlifes sipping tasteless lager and chomping on grey meat pies. A far cry from the 'Crocodile Dundee' stereotype of Aussie manhood.

The only respectable places in the cities for wholesome social drinking and entertainment are RSLs (ex-service clubs) where the profits go into bowling greens and supporting cricket. Many large, Art Deco Suburban cinemas built in Sydney and the surrounding metropolis in the 1930s, have been quietly taken over by these antipodean working men's clubs where old 'silver screen' stages now house banks of hundreds of shiny pokies constantly fed by Dame Edna lookalikes.

Whenever I could, I would get out of Sydney and head back to the countryside that I was born in and loved, the wide-open plains and mountains beyond the Great Dividing Range. I had a go at most jobs and was never short of work – but writing, and yarning about writing, was far easier for me. I picked up the name "Banjo" not because I was much of a player, but because my favourite horse had that name. I loved that old horse, he was a real beaut. I told all kinds of stories about him, so much so my mates called me Banjo and that name just stuck.

In the end I packed in the lawyering to become a full-time writer and journalist. I returned to my roots, regularly travelling out in the great open spaces. As I roamed the outback, mixing with the drovers and Bush folk, visiting my extended farming family, I picked up new stories, wrote poetry, sang songs by the campfire, and drank a bit on occasion! One folk song that I put together became so popular, such a big hit in fact, that it became the very first popular anthem in Australia and ultimately, in the British Empire.

I wrote "Waltzing Matilda" in January 1895 while staying at a sheep and cattle station in Winton, Queensland, owned by friends – the Macpherson family. I'd heard a local story from the family, and thought I could write some words to it. I wrote the first verse, tried it out, and thought it went down well. I wrote the other verses, and put the words to a little Scottish tune I'd heard their daughter, Christina, play on a zither. She in turn had heard the tune played as a march by a military band. I decided the music would be good to set lyrics to, and managed to finish the complete story-set-to-song during the rest of my stay.

It has been widely accepted that "Waltzing Matilda" is probably based on events in Queensland in 1891 when the 'Great Shearers Strike' brought the colony close to civil war. It was broken only after the Premier of Queensland called in the military. In September 1894, some shearers again went on strike. The situation turned violent, with the striking shearers firing their rifles and pistols in the air and setting fire to the woolshed, killing dozens of sheep. The owner of Sheep Station and three policemen gave chase to one of the men named Sam Hoffmeister. Rather than be captured, Sam shot and killed himself at a nearby waterhole.

I ended up making a living as a journalist and writer of all kinds of books, articles, songs and ballads. I picked up the nickname 'The Man From Snowy Mountains' from the title of a book I wrote. It was a bit of a mystery to me, seeing as my native Orange is in the middle of the blessed prairie, but publicists were then, are now, and possibly always will be a bunch of 'drongoes'!"

BP's writing, particularly "The Man from Snowy Mountain" became very popular in Australia and even in England, where critics compared BPs output favourably with Rudyard Kipling's works. BP gradually worked more in ballad and poem writing, and journalism.

In 1898, when the British Empire picked a fight with the Boers, I packed up my kit and headed off to become a war correspondent just for adventure, 'the hell of it'. I travelled with a small Australian Army contingent and spent nine months on a horse in the thick of the conflict, daily witnessing really tragic and really wicked events, mostly brought on by the actions of the British Army. I picked up lots of compliments for my writing though – even from the Poms. So much so, that reporting got into my blood and after the war was settled I decided to continue. I explored China on horseback, reporting as I went.

I returned to Sydney to become a Newspaper editor after an unsuccessful dabble in farming. I lost a pack of money for my efforts – I hadn't got my old man's rugged temperament to stick with the varied challenges of the ever-changing Aussie weather and the cut-throat capitalism of colonial life. Settling down meant that I got happily married to Alice Emily. She was the daughter of farming folk too, she sorted me out, always understood my passions, and we were blessed with a great pair of kids.

When the Great War began I just had to go to Europe along with, it seemed, every other able-bodied bloke in New South Wales. At first, I worked as a reporter, but then as an ambulance man in the trenches. Later I became a Cavalry man too, until I was badly injured and had to be hospitalised. While I rested, I trained myself up as a vet to look after the horses, and at the ripe old age of fifty-six, they made me into a cavalry major.

Through all those vile conflicts in Europe and the Middle-East my old song 'Waltzing Matilda' echoed around the Aussie contingents, and I was absolutely made-up when it was adopted by all the 'diggers' as their rallying song, and recognised as our unofficial National Anthem!

In the trenches on the "Western Front" Aussie Officers delivered readings to their soldiers from BP's 'Snowy Mountain' stories as relief and for inspiration! Conscripts from Australia's slums, shanty towns, and mines were turned into rugged fearless soldiers by the 'settler folklore' and those who returned from the European conflicts became the new, more self-assured, working class of NSW – resentful of their capitalist bosses who were now equated with the English Officer Class.

Returning to Australia I had a delightful life being a journalist and writing books. I became one of the first radio reporters in NSW. Most often, I could be heard extolling the beauty of this beloved country of mine, which I just wanted to share with everyone. I had a relaxing social life in Sydney and occasionally enjoyed the odd 'deep Sinker' with my mates at the local club.

After the war BP resumed journalism; he contributed to the Sydney Mail and Smith's Weekly and in 1922 became editor of the racing journal, the Sydney Sportsman—an appointment he found very congenial. He retired from active journalism in 1930 to devote his leisure-time to creative writing. He was by now a celebrated and respected citizen of Sydney, most often seen at the elite 'Australian Club' where he had long been a member, and where his portrait now hangs. In following years, he became a successful broadcaster with the Australian Broadcasting Commission talking about his travels and experiences.

As the years passed, I realised that the tales that I wrote, and the ballads that I composed and sang, tapped into some national feeling. It was amazing to be part of something which, eventually, helped shape the national character, and which sustained us through those desperately tough, lean, hard years between the wars when we were all 'down on our uppers'.

In the 1930s Australia was still carrying a double burden. The loss of, or injury to, a huge proportion of its young men in WW1, along with extremely high levels of poverty and recession, was aggravated by the punitive repayment of 'war loans' imposed by Churchill's government to pay and clothe the Colonial troops. Britain had billed Australia for every penny spent on the upkeep of Aussie troops, from their day of enlistment, until they were discharged. All the other Dominions had been relieved of these costs from the moment their soldiers had embarked for war service overseas. These loans continued to be paid by the Australian people into the mid-thirties (long after the British had waived debts from the Germans and French). A revolution was threatened in the mid-thirties in NSW, which was only averted by the threat of federal troops taking over. No wonder so many old-time Aussies despised and mocked the 'bloody Poms' for treating their countrymen so badly, almost to the point of insurrection.

These days Aussies are known, and respected, for our sporting achievements, and our presumed ruthless attitude to football in its various formats, and even in Cricket – where 'Waltzing Matilda' constantly blares out wherever and whenever we win. I guess that's why Europeans think of us as a really stroppy bunch of blokes, even though we are now 'patsies' – our consumption of wine overtook our beer drinking decades ago.

Who would have ever guessed that I, Banjo Patterson, would have topped the list as number one of "The Greatest Ever Australians" in 2013 almost seventy-two years after my death. Certainly not me! All I ever wanted was to ride a good horse and spin a good yarn.

'The Greatest of All - Our 50 Top Australians' was a newspaper article published in The Australian on 27 June 2013, coinciding with that year's National Australia Day.

1. **Banjo Paterson**: Bush poet (born 1864, New South Wales; died 1941, New South Wales)
2. **Sir Donald Bradman**: Cricketer (born 1908, NSW; died 2001, South Australia)
3. **Howard Florey**: Microbiologist, Nobel Prize laureate and one of the discoverers of penicillin (born 1898, South Australia; died 1968, England)
4. **John Curtin**: Australian Prime Minister during the Second World War
5. **St Mary of the Cross MacKillop**: Saint, nun and co-founder of rural education order Sisters of St Joseph of the Sacred Heart (born 1842, NSW; died 1929, NSW)

* * *

48. **Reg Grundy**: T.V.("Neighbours") entrepreneur (born 1923, NSW; died 2016, Bermuda)
49. **Fred Hollows**: Ophthalmologist and humanitarian (born 1929, New Zealand; died 1993, New South Wales)
50. **Richie Benaud**: Cricketer (born 1930, NSW; died 2015, NSW)

The Wall

By Valerie Tyler

Sun shines on orange bricks, casts shadows in crevices
Not seen in blackness, becoming the dark.
The parts in between, never noticed when seen,
Just like cold benches alone in the park,
Where hungry souls sit, and old women knit
Warm jumpers for those without any clothes.
Poor feed the poor who don't own a door.
Their future is stark.
Nowhere to crawl, surrounded by wall.
Hands of the mind, reach out to be kind
Hearing them cry, and wondering why
No-one is listening.

Timepiece

By Jessica Joy

They met on the Tube. He squeezed into the empty seat beside her. Kaylah shifted slightly, but their legs touched with a frisson of electricity. He tucked his bag behind his calves and settled back into the seat. She watched him every day on the platform, but this was the first time he had sat next to her. She stared at the poems and adverts printed on the curved ceiling of the carriage and shifted in her seat, using each fidget to hide her sideways appraisal; the tiny scar on his left eyebrow, the freckle on his ear, the way he played with the hair under his lip as he read.

With the poise of a courtesan, she let her scarf slip down her leg to his shoe. She stole a look at him, ready to smile and apologise from behind her fanned magazine, but engrossed in his book, he didn't seem to notice. Her heart quickened and she turned her head towards him to breathe in the faint aroma of sandalwood and musk. She wanted to link her arm through his, lie her head on his shoulder, and listen to the sound of his breathing, for ever.

The green and white ceramic tiles of her station came into focus through the windows as the train slowed to a stop. With a twinge of regret, she made her way to the door and glanced back over her shoulder. The doors hissed open, but he was busy checking the station name through the window and did not look her way. She stepped onto the platform and was lost in the crowd. She joined the heaving throng of commuters. They bustled and shoved, teeming towards the light, a swarm of hungry rats jostling through the sewers of the underground, driven by the collective consciousness; *work-home, home-work, work-home*. Kaylah was tired, bored, lonely, and something had to change. Maybe it was time to use the time machine?

At home, she rummaged through the clutter in the attic for the small wooden box that contained the Timepiece, letter, and instructions from her mother.

The letter was explicit, 'If you ever need to use the Timepiece, please do so with extreme caution. With time travel comes great responsibility: there are ALWAYS consequences, however careful you try to be. You get ONE use only, so please choose wisely. I hope, from the bottom of my heart, you never need to use it.' Kaylah turned the Timepiece over in her palm. It was a large, heavy, silver fob watch with a beautiful case and ornate engravings that looked like planets in orbit. The face of the watch was complicated, like a diver's watch; there were three smaller dials and what appeared to be corresponding crowns and pushers to change the settings. She read the instructions several times and then held her breath as she set the dials and pushed the crown.

On reflection, she may have been impetuous. She was back on the Tube, next to Charlie. She had touched his leg as she picked up her scarf, started a conversation and asked him about his book. Names and numbers were exchanged. That was the start of Kaylah and Charlie. That was the start of a love affair she could only dream about until then. That was five years ago.

This morning had played out like any other morning; warm pyjamas crumpled behind the knees, hot tea and crumpets dripping with butter, an invitation to their friend's wedding in the post and a text from Charlie confirming his flight should land in an hour and he would get a taxi from the airport.

Now Kaylah sat and stared at the empty hospital bed. The morning sun had moved across the sky and filled the room with an orange glow as it sank behind the city skyline. *No time to say goodbye. There's never enough time. Time is of the essence. If I could turn back time.* She hadn't cried this hard since – since ever. She had asked the nurse for a little more time and, ironically, had been told to take all the time she needed. What she needed was Charlie, back, alive. What she needed was Charlie in a different taxi, on a different road, nowhere near a jack-knifed lorry.

They hadn't stripped the bed yet and there were smears of blood and other fluids from his poor, spent body, on the sheet. The pale-blue, waffle blanket lay in a heap at the end of the bed. It had settled neatly over his corpse for a couple of hours, folded under his toned, mottled arms and tucked tightly under the mattress either side; like they had thought his still, empty shell of a body might drift to the ceiling. She had laid her head on his chest one last time and tried to imagine his soft touch brush away her tears. But there was no comfort; the man she adored was gone. She focussed on the imprint his head had left on the pillow and rubbed gentle circles over the taut skin that protected their growing child. She thought of the Timepiece now with contempt. She had already tried the little knobs, shook the fob, tapped the glass, but time had become obstinate and linear. There was no going back again.

* * *

Kaylah sat at the kitchen table with her tea and crumpets. She dripped butter on her pyjamas. She couldn't wait for Charlie to come home later. She missed him so much when he worked away. She smiled to herself as she imagined his head on her bump whispering to the baby and gazing up to wink at her.

She opened the wedding invitation from her friend which was decorated with an orange blossom design and embossed in gold, expensive. The timing was awful; she would either have a new-born or be overdue. Still, she couldn't miss it; they went back years.

There was a knock at the front door. Kaylah groaned as she heaved herself up. The girl at the door looked vaguely familiar.

"Hi, I'm Hannah," she said. "Wow, you look so young."

Kaylah was confused but the girl continued.

"I have a really important message for you. I'm afraid something awful is going to happen to Charlie this afternoon. You have to stop him from getting the taxi at the airport; make sure he gets the train or maybe go and collect him." Kaylah's phone pinged a text alert sound. She stared at the girl speechless.

"Mum, it's me, Hannah," the girl said. "You gave me the Timepiece and a card. Dad dies in a car crash this afternoon unless you stop him getting into that taxi. Please answer his text, now. Please change that."

Kaylah could not take her eyes off the girl. She could see it; the shape of her mother's face, Charlie's gentle eyes, and her own chestnut hair with that maddening cowlick in the fringe. Mouth open in wonder, she picked up the phone and told Charlie she would come and get him, to which he responded with a kiss.

Kaylah stared at her daughter. "You are so beautiful, Hannah." She laughed, "We haven't even decided on that name yet, we don't know if you're a girl or a boy. How old are you? Tell me everything. No wait, don't tell me anything."

"Mum, I have to go. I'm twenty-one. You know the rules." Hannah was fading. "You've spent your whole life blaming yourself for using the Timepiece selfishly. I'm here to put things right." She was almost gone. "And don't bother with a new hat. You don't make it to the wedding, you're too busy having me!"

Kaylah found a pen and turned the wedding invitation over. On the blank side, she scribbled the words she hoped would set things right, that would save her soulmate and protect their family. The message was simple, 'If you ever need to use the Timepiece, please do so with extreme caution. With time travel comes great responsibility: there are ALWAYS consequences, however careful you try to be. You get ONE use only, so please choose wisely. And remember, Hannah, if you light a lamp for somebody, it will also brighten your path.'

WHAT GOES AROUND

BY JOHN EMERY

He was watching, vaguely aware of the falling snow, snow falling so heavily as to remind him of the white-out effects he'd heard about in news reports, of climbers losing their orientation, and lives. Events appeared as if at the end of a tunnel, this he knew was what blocked out all the other stuff which would be fine if it helped focus, but he also knew that blocking out the 'other stuff' meant what he did see was not truly in context. He remembered as a child being taken to an art gallery, people standing back to view a painting, whereas he was drawn to stand as close as possible intrigued by the detail. He should stand back now; he knew that he should see the Man o' War being towed to the ships graveyard and not just a few brush strokes depicting a section of cloud, but oh, that detail, that astonishing detail.

With his vision returning and the snowfall thinning, he saw the cherry trees and the grass punctuated with wild flowers. A blue sky provided a backdrop to a few wisps of white cloud as he had almost reached the boundary of those trees. This was all he had to his world in this moment of time excepting something glimpsed, almost as an imperfection to this picture, a building. Not a grand building, far from it, just an unused stable block situated some way from the large farmhouse with its many other outbuildings. Why should he be thankful of this, why should he even care, why should he feel concern about being as nature intended him to be? It seemed natural. It felt good, it felt very good, this thing people called Naturism. Derek had just recently given up wearing his last item of apparel in these forays. His shoes. The soles of his feet had toughened up now and even the wretched Athletes Foot that used to plague him had given up on him. His feet. "Ah yes," he looked at his feet in all their glory, the snow landing on them and indeed the rest of him and not melting, and why should blossom from the cherry trees melt anyway, especially on a very fine day at the very start of May?

Derek wondered why this day, rather than any other was so firmly set in his memory. He was all too grateful for his wife choosing to live in a bungalow because it saved him the task of climbing up the stairs only to have forgotten why. Of course! That day long ago was set so firm not simply due to his wife, but the Daily Mail she chose to have delivered each day. More to the point that bloody Maggie Thatcher; '*10 years as PM, the first Prime Minister of the 20th century to achieve this*' the Daily Mail harked in its headline article. Yes! It was Maggie who put him in this rage, not his lovely wife; it was Maggie that was the impetus for his 'mood resetting naturist excursion' as he liked to think of it. Too late he made the inevitable connection, bloody Maggie Thatcher causing him to stroll around the orchard in the buff, some kind of Freudian slip perhaps, a distinctly queasy feeling had been thankfully suppressed by thoughts of his wife with a cup of tea and generous portion of chocolate cake waiting for his return, even if she did not eat it herself. His wife, yes, he had proved very fortunate in that part of his life. Most people would comment, on the quiet of course, how he was 'punching well above his weight', which he knew to be true. But that was back then on that day – the fourth of May 1989. Christ. Why should he remember this date when he had difficulty recollecting what he'd eaten for breakfast? He suspected it was probably one of those tricks your memory plays on you after a certain age. Why not? After all his whole body had decided to 'play tricks' on him these days. He was not fond of the particularly mean trick that had resulted in certain parts of his body sagging while other parts grew against his will.

Now so many years later he was retracing his steps trying to relive all this, churn it over in his mind in the hope of making sense of it all. Perhaps this was a 'yin yang' balancing of the scales, the dread of the here and now making up for a wonderful past? Now? Oh yes! Now! How things had changed. The thought was trite. An amazing wife, fourteen years his junior and some few inches taller than himself at almost 6 feet, but with an elegant form that meant she weighed considerably less than him. She cared for the needs of the children, both beautiful blonde boys with just two years between them. She was a wonderful cook, did all the decorating and cared for their extensive garden. Ah, yes, the garden. He would walk to her in the garden, an orange cut into segments on a plate held out as refreshment for her, poor recompense for all she did, but it was a gesture she loved. What did he give in return? Very tricky one this he thought. He supposed that his early 'retirement' from the bank 'with an enhanced pension old chap' gave them a pleasant lifestyle. He also spent rather a lot of time at his club; well it was the bowls club, but it was good enough for him. She even tolerated his returning home for dinner pissed. Yes – 'pissed' was the only fair description of his state after several glasses of his beloved Glenmorangie, and this in her car. The only plus Derek could think of was that it kept him out of her way. No. His side of the balance sheet did not look good, not good at all.

But yesterday, twenty-three years to the day after that harping headline it was not the bloody Daily Mail putting him in a blind rage. It was the saying goodbye to his beautiful wife. He felt the urge to retch at the thought of her being the first to go, at the unfairness of it. This was not looking through 'a tunnel at the detail'. This was wide angle, panoramic vile technicolour, and it was most definitely not fair, not fair at all.

A gunshot made him start; he hadn't noticed how far he had walked. Rabbits? Rabbits were the scourge of the arable farmer. The beautiful cherry orchard had long since been grubbed out, taking with it the wildlife and flowers. Now it was just wheat and if you were lucky, the chrome yellow of rape. A desert bereft of the beautiful detail he adored, and no longer offering reasonable possibilities for his naturist ramblings. Not that these held the same allure at an age when body parts were so determined to head south. Crisp mornings that would once have been invigorating stabbed through the flesh and into his old bones. There would be no wife awaiting his return with a cup of tea and a slab of chocolate cake covered in toasted coconut. His wife had never joined him, even in the early days. He didn't mind this, he was proud of his wife and her beauty and had no intention of sharing it with anyone else, however minimal the chance of encountering anyone in that orchard. It was only now, when it was too late, he realised what a stupid unreformed twit he had been to turn down her offer of lovemaking amongst the wild flowers.

Another gunshot, no two this time. For one little rabbit? He considered the cost of cartridges or whatever they were called. He had long held the opinion that the killing of wildlife was some perverse sense of fun rather than commercial prudence. He took stock of his surroundings and to his delight he had managed to retrace his path from all those years ago without encountering either a dead rabbit or the farmer with his 'gun, gun, gun'. If only he could shake off the indigestion. He couldn't blame it on the chocolate cake. Derek pulled his coat around him. What thin sunlight there had been was now gone and the chill seemed eager to find its way to his old bones. He felt strangely sweaty. He'd walked this way so many times before in all kinds of weathers, times and moods, how on earth had he not spotted what he was now looking at? Was it the sudden jolt of the gunshot, the cruel chill of the wind, or perhaps that he now found himself alone, almost unguarded? Was it this that made him notice the dull, aching pain in his left arm? He spotted that a line of trees had been felled and here was the notice from the council 'To remove row of Elder trees'. Bloody weeds of the tree world. He pressed on, despite feeling breathless, feeling old, but not ready to give up yet. Always a person to take the easy option, this compulsion was a new sensation to him, he was being drawn to something, a destiny of kinds. Perhaps this was the cause of this sensation of light-headedness.

Now that the trees had been removed a rather elegant, pretty cottage was revealed. How had this been built in a conservation area without general knowledge? Even as he thought this the penny was dropping. This was where the stable had stood, no, still stands, but now as if morphed into a very pleasing house for a family. Awareness of that disused stable had been lost by the cover of the rapidly growing elder trees. Those trees had now had their day, even the stumps had been ground away leaving nothing to show of them. This pleasant thought wasn't enough to take his mind off the pain he now had in his neck. No, his jaw. Damn! He really was getting old. His eyes drawn to the reawakened stables he noticed a rather tall, comely young woman who looked strangely familiar. Maybe it was the grubby hands from working in the garden. Fussing around her were two children at her side, young boys, both blonde with just a couple of years to separate them. Was he truly sure of this? His view of his surroundings had changed and he was looking through whiteness, a tunnel, a tube of sorts. He watched as they all turned rapidly to face the house. A man entered the garden. He was shorter than her, and certainly thicker around the waist. He bore a striking resemblance to himself when younger. He was feeling truly out of sorts now, seeing events through a white tunnel. He felt himself, falling, falling through the whiteness, towards the husband, the husband holding out something for his wife on a plate. Seeing now, through the whiteness as the falling stopped, a plate, and on the plate a segmented orange.

I Belong To Inspirations Writers' Group . . .

. . . because it's a place to share, improve and write. There is a mixed bag of writerly experience across different literature genres. Most importantly it's a place of energy and vitality, attended by warm and friendly people.

Anna Spain

. . . because being there focuses me, provides support, keeps me motivated and ups my game. Plus Carol brings nice biscuits – worth attending just for those alone!

Anne Sikora Lord

I set up Inspirations Writing Group . . . because, writing for me, is an incredibly lonely occupation. I found submitting work to agents and publishers, and being rejected, time after time, soul-destroying. I needed the support of others, like me, who wrote without reward, and I found them here. Inspirations maintains my sanity.

Carol Salter

. . . because I have always enjoyed writing and wanted to get inspiration to develop this further – and a passion for tea and biscuits runs in the family!

Claire Meakins

. . . because it's nice to hang out with such a varied, interesting, well-balanced and fruitful crop.

David Morrish

. . . because I enjoy meeting like-minded people in a relaxed group, and hearing about local writing-related events.

Elizabeth Lee

. . . because talking to fellow writers spurs me on and teaches me a lot.

Ellen Carli

. . . because it is indeed inspirational!

Ernestina Fetissova

. . . to share and exchange thoughts, work, ideas and aspirations with fellow writers.

Jessica Joy

. . . because with such a diverse mix of talented people, inspiration is just what you get.

John Emery

. . . because I enjoy the warmth, support and encouragement. I always learn something myself, and hopefully help others.

Karen Ince

. . . because I've found my play group, where we love words and what they can do.

Karen Leopold Reich

. . . because it is made up of supportive writers who work well together. As a writer, I feel less isolated and more inspired by the energy the group as a whole generates.

Kim Hammond

. . . because I love the friendship of other writers.

Lee Russell

. . . because I love writing, but I know that inspiration is not always easy to find. The support and sometimes criticism of other writers, many of whom are experiencing similar challenges to myself, will help me to become the writer I would like to be.

Mary Gumsley

. . . because the fellow members are supportive and friendly, which makes learning simply a joy.

Niki Sakka

. . . . originally to accompany my daughter, but I stayed on for the fabulous array of biscuits – and the opportunities to improve my writing and be with fellow writers!

Sarah Meakins

. . . because I like to share ideas and encourage creativity in others, and I have found people to do that with.

Sinead le Blond

. . . because it feeds my imagination and keeps my writing ambitions alive. I value the robust and constructive feedback I receive and am developing my own critiquing skills by reading the work of fellow writers. I discover and develop my own writer voice, and leave each meeting believing that I am a writer. Without the mutual support, respect and friendships that have taken root at the group, I would give up this writing habit, but continue the walks along the sea front talking to myself.

Susan Emm

. . . because my love for creating characters and stories started at an early age. My motivation and confidence came later, and there was lots I needed to learn about writing. Surrounding myself with other writers has helped me to flourish. It is a pleasure to be part of this group and be included in this anthology.

Tracy Jacobs

. . . because it's full of enthusiasm, stimulates individuals' imagination, and inspires our confidence to write.

Tricia Brady

. . . because I enjoy the company of like-minded people in a place which offers progression for writers at different stages, and where there's plenty of support, shared ideas, and of course much inspiration.

Valerie Tyler

ACKNOWLEDGEMENTS

Our thanks go to the following people:

All the writers who make the group such a lively, diverse and encouraging place, whether their work is included in this current volume or not.

Westgate Library for providing us with a place to meet, talk, read work out loud, and drink tea (or coffee) every month.

Carol Salter, for setting up and running the group, always welcoming new members, and encouraging everyone to be the best writer they can be. For all her hard work in collating submissions for this anthology, and the multiple rounds of sending it out for critique and back to the writer for revision. For her patience and good humour.

All members of the group who helped with critiquing the writing included here.

Karen Ince for proof-editing and formatting the collection, and for the cover design.